WILD IN RIO

LYSSA KAY ADAMS

LKA PUBLISHING

P.O. Box 368

Williamston, MI 48895

Publisher's note: This is a work of fiction. Names, characters, places, and incidents are a product of the author's imagination. Locales and public names are sometimes used for atmospheric purposes. Any resemblance to real people, living or dead, or to businesses, companies, events, institutions, or locales is completely coincidental.

ISBN: 978-0-9974035-2-7

❀ Created with Vellum

PROLOGUE

Two years ago
Galway, Ireland

{PADRAIG}

There are fish in the sea better than have ever been caught.

That's an old Irish saying, one I only know it because it was embroidered on a towel that served as a makeshift curtain over the cracked bathroom window in the shithole Dublin flat where I spent the first six years of life.

I don't know how the towel got there or who hung it. It probably came with the apartment when we moved in, left behind by some other bloke who snorted the rent or gambled away the grocery money. I just know it was always there, frayed and soiled, something to stare at while I sat on the john or hid in the tub with my hands over my ears, pretending I couldn't hear what was happening in the rooms beyond. I read it so many times as a kid that the words became nothing more than meaningless shapes and empty sounds.

Most of my childhood memories are like that—empty flickering images, like papers tossed into the breeze. Random and impossible to catch, always floating just out of reach.

But that towel, that saying … that's a memory I can grab with both hands. And as I round the corner to the street overlooking the bay—the puppies yipping and yanking on their leashes—the voice in my head digs the words from the recess in my brain where I store such things.

There are fish in the sea better than have ever been caught.

Suddenly it means something.

Because suddenly I see her.

She's alone on a bench, staring motionless at the water. The wicked wind off the shore whips her long, dark hair from her shoulders, but she seems to barely notice. Even from this distance, I can tell she's crying.

Not the sobbing kind of crying—you know, the kind that comes from a sudden gut-punch of emotion that sends you doubling over, and you hope someone is there to catch you.

It's the quiet kind of crying, the kind where you just sit and let the tears fall because there's nothing left to do. The kind you do alone.

I've done both.

The quiet kind is worse.

I jerk to a halt so quickly that even the dogs are startled into obedience. For five blocks, I've muttered every feckin' curse word I know. I've cursed my boxing coach for guilting me into helping his niece with her dogs this week. I've cursed the puppies for not knowing how to run in a straight line or piss without getting it all over themselves. Mostly, I've cursed myself for needing the money so badly that even walking a pack of unruly Border Collie puppies during the annual Galway horse festival is something I can't turn down.

The only thing I'm cursing right now, though, is that I have no idea what to do about the beautiful, sad girl staring at the water like she's waiting for answers.

Like all she has left is the hope there are fish in the sea better than the ones she's caught so far in life.

One of the puppies spots a bird and lets out an excited bark. The girl's head jerks in my direction, and then just as quickly, jerks away. Her hands fly to her face as she wipes away her tears.

"I'm sorry," I say, letting the dogs pull me closer. "I didn't mean to startle ya'."

She stands, keeping her face down. "No, it's fine."

Her accent is American. In town for the festival, probably.

"I was just … I was just admiring the view," she says.

So am I. Because the closer I get, the more the air seeps from my lungs. She's hypnotically beautiful. Like, the kind of pretty that inspires poetry and makes me wish I had paid more attention when the nuns taught about James Joyce and Yeats. Never thought I'd have much use in my life for fine literature, but I need better words right now to describe her.

She's younger than me but not by much. Early twenties, I'm guessing. No ring on her finger.

She won't look at me, but she smiles at the dogs with genuine warmth. "Looks like you have your hands full."

"Yeah, they're a right rowdy bunch."

She drops to one knee and lets the puppies swarm her. A spot of joy pushes away some of the clouds in her expression, and an honest-to-God giggle escapes her lips as one puppy leaps to lick her face.

"Border Collies are such good dogs. Are you selling them?"

"No, uh, they're not mine. I'm just helpin' out a friend. She's sellin' them, though, if you're interested. I mean, I don't know how that works, you being American and all. Can you buy a dog in a foreign country?"

Fer fuck's sake, could I babble anymore?

The smile evaporates from her face. I wonder if she knows she's clutching the puppy to her chest. The pup doesn't seem to mind, though. He's lax against her and falling in love. I'm not sure I can blame him.

"Look, it's none of my business, but are you all right?"

"What?" She looks up, surprised. "Oh, yes. I'm fine." She gives a nervous little laugh and waves her hand at nothing. "Sorry. My, um, my eyes get watery in the wind."

I crouch down next to her.

"Aye," I say, trying to keep my tone gentle, because she's as skittish as a club fighter facing a champion in the ring. "What's wrong?"

Her fingers dig into the puppy's fur, mindlessly massaging behind his ears as her eyes get a faraway gaze to them.

"I'm not trying to pry. It's just, when I saw you sitting here—"

"Do you think you're ever too old to run away from home?"

Um, OK. Wow. That's a right hook straight in the feels. "Guess that would depend on what you're running away from," I say cautiously. "And why."

Listen to me. Man of wisdom. As if my own life isn't a speeding train headed for a cliff of my own making. But she seems to be considering my words, so … "Is that why you're sitting here all alone? You're running away?"

She blinks rapidly and releases the pup. It protests with a whimper, and I wince in sympathy. *Sorry, mate.*

"I should go," she says, standing.

"Are you sure you're all right?" I jump to my feet. "Can I walk you somewhere?"

"Thank you, but I'm OK. I just—" She sucks in a deep, shaky breath. "I just have some decisions I need to make."

"They must be tough ones."

She dips her chin in a crisp nod. Then, with a shy smile that doesn't quite reach her eyes, she turns to walk away.

I act without thinking. "Wait."

She turns around. I dig into my pocket, wrap my fingers around the smooth stone that has walked with me since I was seventeen, and hand it to her.

"I don't know about running away," I say, folding it into her long fingers. "But I do believe it's never too late to start over."

Surprise bleeds into confusion as she shifts her gaze from me to the stone in her palm. Her thumb traces the etching of two hands cradling a heart and a crown.

"What is this?" she breathes.

"It's the Claddagh. Irish symbol for friendship."

"No, I mean …" She meets my eyes. "Why are you giving me this?"

And now I feel like an eejit. My cheeks burn. "It's, uh, it's nothing."

"It's not nothing. You were carrying it in your pocket."

"It's just a good luck charm someone gave me once," I shrug.

"Someone important?"

It's my turn to nod, even as I fight a tightening sensation in my throat I really don't fuckin' like.

"And now you're giving it to me? A stranger?"

"You don't really feel like a stranger."

Her eyes grow wide as I blurt out the truest sentence I've ever said, but then her lips begin to tremble.

"Ah, shite, I'm sorry. It was stupid. I just—"

"Thank you," she says, her voice thick and her eyes glistening. "This is honestly the kindest thing anyone has ever done for me."

And before I realize what's happening, she rises on tiptoe, leans in to me, and presses her lips to my bearded cheek. It lands straight in my heart.

"Who are you?" I whisper.

She shakes her head and steps away. In all my life, I've never seen a smile so sad.

"I'm nobody."

1

2016

Rio de Janeiro

{EVER}

"YOU'RE HER, YES?"

I hear the voice—a heavy French accent—before I register that it's directed at me. I look up from my place in line in the dining hall of the athlete's village to find a pair of grinning Frenchmen staring at me. One holds a phone with the screen facing out.

My own image stares back at me.

"I'm sorry," I stammer. "What?"

"Ever Beckinsale," he says, pointing at my face. "Twenty hottest Americans."

Seriously? I haven't even been in Rio for half a day, and already someone is throwing that in my face?

One of the French dudes waggles his eyebrows in what he apparently thinks is suggestive. But what *he* thinks it suggests and what *I* think it suggests are clearly two different things, because I kind of want to puke in my mouth.

That stupid CelebrityBuzz list has been the bane of my existence ever since it was posted three days ago. *Twenty hottest American athletes to follow in Rio.* Yeah, that is *exactly* what I need leading to the most important competition of my life—one more thing my critics can point to as some kind of evidence that I'm not the real deal.

I'm one of the youngest Americans ever to qualify for the national equestrian team in show jumping, which for anyone else would be an unquestionable achievement. But since my rise in the sport has been rapid by equestrian standards, combined with the fact that I also happen to be the heiress to the global Beckinsale hotel chain, my presence in Rio is apparently suspect.

Daddy must have bought her a spot on the team. People are actually saying that about me. As if my competition victories mean nothing. As if I haven't sacrificed every semblance of a normal life —college, friendships, love, *sex*—to get here. As if I didn't have to make a painful choice two years ago for which I'm still paying the price.

As if my father would actually part with the money.

That's the funniest thing about it. The only thing Mitchell Beckinsale would pay for would be to keep me *off* the team.

It doesn't matter, though. In sixteen days, I will take my place on that podium and prove them all wrong. Especially my parents.

But first, I have a pair of clueless Frenchmen to deal with.

"It's me," I finally say, tugging my USA ball cap lower on my brow, hoping they get the hint.

They don't.

The one with the eyebrows grasps my hand. "Mon amour, j'ai hâte de te voir sur tes genoux," he croons, pressing his lips to my knuckles.

My love, you are going to look so good on your knees.

"Je préférerais faire la pipe à une chèvre," I fire back, pulling my hand away.

Their mouths drop open as red splotches rise on their cheeks. Then they spin on their heels and storm off.

Huh. Guess they were offended that I would rather blow a goat.

A soft clap sounds behind me.

"Well, that was bloody brilliant," an Irish brogue laughs.

I suck in a gasp—an automatic response whenever I hear an Irish accent. I turn around to find a crooked smile and an outstretched hand.

"Lorna O'Toole," the young woman says. "Irish rowin' team."

I grip her hand for a quick shake. "Ever Beckinsale. American show jumper."

"Yeah, I heard that. And one of the hottest Americans, apparently, yeah?"

I groan out loud this time. "It's so embarrassing."

"I'd be adding that to my badge, if I were you. The lads will be linin' up."

"I don't *want* them to line up."

"Then how 'bout you let me hang with you, and you can just hand them off to me?"

I laugh. "Deal."

The line inches forward, and I'm starting to wonder if I'd be better off just eating one of the granola bars in my room. A limp salad and a warm smoothie can't possibly be worth this wait. Lorna must have noticed the desperate, hungry look on my face, because she pats my arm.

"Don't worry. It's only like this on the first day or so. Once everyone gets settled into their training schedules and competition begins, things calm down and it won't take so long."

"You've been to the Olympics before?"

She nods. "London."

I glance around and drop my voice. "Is it all true, what they say?"

Sex is supposedly the universal sport here. Organizers apparently ordered more than four hundred thousand condoms to hand out just for the athletes. If previous media reports are true, it won't be long before people start hooking up right out in the open.

Lorna's grin stretches her cheeks wide. "Oh, it's true. It's not the summer games, darlin'. It's the shaggin' games."

I laugh again and shake my head. "I might have to hide in my room the entire time."

"No way. I won't let ya'. In fact, some of the lads on the boxing team are having a party tonight in their room. Bring yourself and make me look good."

My mind scrambles for an excuse. I'm usually pretty good at coming up with reasons to cover my natural inclination toward all things anti-social, but I can't think of anything that won't sound totally lame.

"Sure," I finally say, fingers mentally crossed. it's not like I actually have to go. "What room?"

"Tenth floor. Room ten twenty-eight. Around eight o'clock sound good?"

I nod and start to reply, but a buzzing in my pocket cuts me off. "Sorry. Excuse me for one second?"

I pull my phone out and glance at the screen. My stomach sinks to my shoes.

My father.

I knew I would have to talk to him eventually, but I'm not ready. For a split second, I consider declining the call, but if I don't answer now, I'll just be delaying the inevitable.

I swear I can hear the theme to Jaws as I swipe my thumb across the screen. "Hi, Dad."

"I wasn't sure if you'd answer."

Subtext for the uninitiated: *I'm surprised you didn't disappoint me.*

"Hang on a second." I pull the phone away from ear and smile at Lorna.

"It was nice meeting you," I say. "I guess I'll have to skip the salad."

She waves. "Nice meetin' you, too. See you at the party, yeah?"

I nod as I duck out of line and then press the phone to my ear again. "I'm back."

"Good. Your mother and I want to talk to you again about your housing situation."

Of course. Right to the point. No, *How was the flight?* Or, *Did you get checked in OK?* Or even, *Sorry for kicking you out and selling your horses. No hard feelings?*

Right. I'll be waiting for that one for a long time.

I sigh and weave through a surging mass of track-suit-wearing athletes checking out each other's assets. "There's nothing I can do about it."

"That's not true. That tennis player is staying outside the village in a rented house. So are some of the basketball players. Why can't you?"

"They get special waivers because they're mega superstars and get swarmed by people wanting autographs the minute they step foot inside the village. I don't exactly meet that standard."

"You're a Beckinsale."

He says it like that should say it all. And to him, it does. In his world, being a Beckinsale is like being God.

I push through another clog of athletes, keeping my head low to avoid anyone else recognizing me. It's no less crowded or quieter in the outer lobby.

"I don't want you staying in that village, Ever. It's indecent and, frankly, beneath us. Your mother and I have rented an enormous villa overlooking the ocean. There's no logical reason for you to not stay there."

"Except that it's against the rules." *And except for the fact that I would rather shove a fork in my eye than spend a single night in the same house as you.*

"Who do I need to talk to about this?"

"No one. And even if you could, I'm an adult. It would be my decision anyway."

Dad makes a noise in the back of his throat—the one he makes whenever he's faced with the inconvenient reminder that money can't buy everything. Especially his daughter.

"Why do you always have to be so difficult?" he growls.

"I'm not being difficult, Dad. I'm just establishing my own rules."

"Did your shrink teach you to say that?"

"You know what? I think it would be best if you and Mom don't come to Rio. Not if it's going to be like this."

"And how would it look to the world if we weren't there?"

"At least it would stop people from saying that you paid off the selection committee."

Silence. I can picture him struggling to gain control—nostrils flared, stance wide, jaw clenched. His posturing used to make me cower and hide as a child. Not anymore.

"This trip isn't just about you, Ever. I've lined up several important business meetings. Brazil is a market we've been wanting to break into, so it kills two birds with one stone."

Ah. There it is. He'll play the proud father bit if it can make him money.

My mother's voice rises in the background. "Let me talk to her."

Oh, yay. They're ganging up on me. A moment passes, and then she replaces my dad on the line.

"Darling, we just have your best interests at heart. You know that, don't you? It's just that Rio is so ... so *dirty.*"

"We're not living in shacks, Mom. The condos are brand new."

"Will you at least come to one of the dinners we have planned?"

"I don't know. We're on a pretty tight leash."

"I hardly think one dinner is out of the question," Mom says. "You are still part of this family, whether you want to be or not."

You're the ones who pushed me out. The words are on the tip of my tongue, but I don't say them. There's no point anymore.

I lean against the wall and reach inside my pocket. The smooth stone is instant comfort—a warm, anchoring weight. Not a single day has passed in the two years since he gave it to me that I haven't thought of him, my mystery man of Ireland.

Even during the worst of it—when my father actually made good on his threat to throw me out and cut me off after I ended my engagement, or worse, when I arrived one day to find the stables locked and my horses gone—even then, I could close my eyes and remember a sincere smile, a gentle voice, and a kind gesture just by running my fingers over the etching. And that would give me the courage to keep going.

He told me the Claddagh was the symbol of friendship, but to me, it has come to mean strength. And if it takes me the rest of my life, I will find him, and I will thank him. Whoever he is.

I steel my spine, returning my attention to my mom. "When?"

"The most important one is with the head of Brazil's tourism bureau. That's on the fifteenth."

That's day after the qualifying round. My parents must have some confidence in my abilities, or else they wouldn't have scheduled anything beyond the fourteenth.

"Fine," I say. I can handle *one* dinner. "I'll be there."

"Good. Now, we get in early Friday. Thank God your father bought us that new plane ..."

I tune out my mother as she raves about how the new plane has a bed, and the VIP seats they got for the opening ceremony, and the *lovely* Armani outfit she bought for the occasion. And, oh! Did I hear that Paige Worthington is getting married? They'd better hurry, though, if they want to book the Waldorf-Astoria because, can you believe they're actually closing it?

I listen with half an ear as my mother babbles, verbal proof that in some circles, money does buy happiness. If Blair Beckinsale had to live like the rest of the world for even a day—hell, if she had to attempt to live like *me*—she'd throw herself off the nearest bridge.

"That sounds great, Mom," I finally interrupt. "Listen, I have to run. Text me when you get in, OK?"

I end the call over her protests and lean my head against the wall behind me, eyes closed.

"Still hungry?"

I open my eyes. Lorna stands in front of me holding a pair of to-go salads and a drink carrier with pink smoothies.

"Starving," I smile.

Lorna nods toward an outdoor dining patio. "Then let's go eat."

I trail after her feeling like the new kid in school who just made her first friend. We find a spot in the shade, and Lorna has me in stitches almost immediately talking about the antics of the last games.

That's when it hits me. I'm really here. I really did it. I've been focused on this moment for as long as I can remember. Eight hours in the saddle every single day, seven days a week. It has all been for this—the chance to prove to myself I can do this, and the chance to prove to my parents they were wrong. This wasn't a waste of time. My life's passion wasn't the worthless pursuit they always said it was.

And next month, when I finally have access to the trust fund my grandparents left me—the one my father can't touch—my life will officially be my own.

This is the beginning of my fresh start.

And you know what?

I'm starting with that party tonight.

2

{PADRAIG}

IF I HADN'T JUST SPENT the past two hours sparring and pounding the mitts, I'd be laying out my roommate on his no-good, fuckin' arse. We've been in Rio all of eight hours, and he's already pulling this shite?

"No fuckin' way, Quinn. We're not having a party in here tonight."

"Come on, Paddy," Quinn says, shoving beers into the refrigerator of our small kitchen. We're sharing a two-bedroom condo, and I'm starting to wish I'd insisted on a single.

"No," I say again.

"We've got three days until competition starts."

"And I'm not spending 'em getting plastered."

Quinn shrugs one shoulder. "So don't drink."

"I said no, Quinn."

"Too late. The lasses will arrive any time. And Lorna says she invited some hot American, too."

I yank the towel from around my neck and stomp to the bathroom for a shower. There's no point arguing with Quinn. He's the only person I know with a bigger stubborn streak than me, which means we're going to get nowhere fast.

I pull open one of the drawers under the sink in search of my shaving kit, but damn near choke at what I find instead. The drawer is filled to the brim with condoms. Quinn must have raided one of the health centers already, but fer fuck's sake, how many women is he planning on shaggin'?

I dig around until I find my razor, and then slam the drawer shut. I can't expect Quinn to understand. This is his first trip to the games. He doesn't know how quickly it all gets away from you—the drinking, the girls, the all-night partying.

He doesn't know what it feels like to come into the games as the gold medal favorite and completely fuck it up because you can't tune out the twin temptations of beer and sex. He doesn't know what it feels like to have to look your coach in the eye and see nothing but disappointment there. He doesn't know what it feels like to have the person who matters most to you in the world put a voice to all your worst doubts.

Are ya' trying to prove people right, lad? You think people are gonna give another chance to a thug from the streets?

I climb in the shower and scrub away the filth from my sparring and the shame of my memories. The London games are over. I won't give my coach or my brother a reason to doubt me ever again. After I won the qualifying round in the heavyweight division for the Rio games, I made them both a solemn vow. No drinking. No partying. And absolutely no women.

By the time I get out of the shower, I can hear voices in the living room outside. I don't have any clean clothes with me in the bathroom, which leaves me with one option—wrap a towel around my waist and try to dart across the hallway to my room without being noticed.

I yank the door open.

And collide with something soft.

We try to right ourselves, but the floor is still slippery. There's no stopping the inevitable. My feet slide out. Her feet slide in. Her arms flail for something to hold onto, and the only thing she finds is me.

Together we fall. Hard. I land on my back with a grunt, and she lands on my chest with an *oof.*

And only then do I realize … my feckin' towel is gone.

She seems to realize it the same time I do, because her whole body tenses. "Oh my God."

She scrambles to get off, but in her scramblin' her knee misses my balls by barely an inch. I wrap my arms around her and squeeze. "Fer fuck's sake, stop your squirmin' before you kill me."

Her body goes even more rigid against me. "I'm sorry."

"Just be careful, yeah?" I soften my tone. "I'm a little exposed here."

Her nervous laugh sends hot puffs of air against my wet skin, and I nearly groan out loud at the telltale tightening in my stones. Just because I'm swearing off women for the games doesn't mean I don't notice them. And I'm not a saint, either. I'm naked with a woman on top of me—a woman who smells like flowers, feels delicate in my hands, and fits like a fuckin' glove between my legs.

"A-are you OK?" she asks, her voice just a whisp of a thing that reminds of the breeze through the trees back home.

"Yeah," I somehow manage to answer. "You?"

She nods, the movement a caress against my collarbone. Christ almighty, I feel it everywhere.

She lifts her head from my chest with another one of those cute little laughs. The next thing I know, she's peering down at me, and I'm looking up at her, and just like that, I've lost all thought because, holy shite...

Holy fucking shite, *It's her.*

Long dark hair frames a face so beautiful it makes my heart stop, just like it did two years ago. Across her nose, a dusting of freckles pop against porcelain skin and set off wide, round eyes as green as the Irish hills.

Eyes that have haunted my dreams.

How is this possible?

"It's you," I breathe, my fingers instinctively tightening against her lower back.

She blinks rapidly, her lashes casting a spray of shadows against her cheeks. Confusion colors her features. She swallows, pulling my eyes to the hot, frantic pulse in her neck. When her tongue darts out and licks her bottom lip, the frustration of two years of unrequited longing flares up like a Taser to my nerves.

My feckin' voice is useless, my brain mush, my emotions locked in a foggy state of incredulous joy, because *it's her.*

Her eyes search my face as her fingers brace against my biceps. "Do-do we know each other?"

Wait. What?

"Jesus, Paddy, it didn't take ya' long."

The girl sucks in a gasp and scrambles off me at the sound of Quinn behind us.

I try to hold on to her, because if I don't, she might disappear again. "Wait—"

Quinn grabs her arm to haul her to her feet, his laughter a cold shower. She looks down at me, flushes a deep red, and spins away, hands over her face. "Oh my God …"

Fuck. FUCK. I'm naked. The girl of my dreams has literally fallen in my lap, and my balls are flapping in the breeze like a pair of coconuts in a tree.

Quinn doubles over laughing and then tosses me a towel. "Fer Christ's sake, Paddy. Cover yourself."

I shoot to my feet and wrap the white terrycloth around my waist, but I'm too late. She's gone. I shove Quinn out of the way and dart into the hallway just in time to see her round the corner back into the living room.

Thoughts fly through my brain so fast I can barely hang on to each one. Who is she? Why is she here? Is it really possible she doesn't remember me? The girl who has lived in my fantasies for two years tackles me in a bathroom out of nowhere but has no clue who I am. Would Fate be that cruel?

"You always knew how to pick 'em, Paddy," Quinn says, slapping a hand on my shoulder. "Rich *and* hot."

I smack his hand away and try to subdue the edge to my voice as I whip back around. "Who is she?"

"Are you serious?!" Quinn pulls out his phone, hammers out something with his thumbs, and waits for it to load. Then he hands it to me, a smirk on his face that just begs for a right hook.

"She might as well be a royal, mate," Quinn says. "And you let her slide right off ya'."

I scan the screen, but my mind doesn't register immediately what I'm reading. *Twenty Hottest American Athletes to Follow in Rio.* I knew she was American—the accent gave it away—but I had no idea she was an athlete.

Then …

Fuck me.

No. It can't be. There has to be a mistake.

She's a feckin' rich girl? I gave away my Claddagh stone to a bona fide *heiress*?

I was wrong. Fate is fuckin' cunt.

3

{PADRAIG}

QUINN TAKES his phone back and tucks it in his pocket. "You sure about this no sex thing?"

I scowl. "I'm sure."

"Tell me you at least got a feel of that fine arse."

My only answer is an obscene gesture as I cross the hallway, stomp into my room, and slam the door. I plant my hands on top of my wet hair and stare at the carpet. This can't be happening.

Ever Beckinsale. That's her name. As in *that* Beckinsale family. Even a knuckle-dragging, beef head from the Irish gutter like me knows who they are.

Which is probably why she has no clue who I am. Men probably fall at her feet every day. Why would she remember me in a sea of nameless, faceless thousands?

A growl erupts from my chest, and I whip my towel across the room. I dig into my suitcase for some shorts and a t-shirt, dress quickly, and then flop onto my bed. My backpack is on the floor next to me. I haul it onto my lap.

My computer boots up at a glacial pace—can't afford a new one yet—and takes even longer to connect to the Wi-Fi. I go straight to Google and type in her name. Yes, I'm a masochist.

The list of results is more than ten pages, but I click on the first headline.

Beckinsale lands spot on Olympic team

June 29, 2016

Lexington, KY—The United States Equestrian Foundation announced Tuesday the 2016 show jumping team for the Rio games.

Four athlete-and-horse combinations will compete for the United States in August at the Deodoro Olympic Equestrian Center in Rio, including 26-year-old Ever Beckinsale—whose young age have led some to question her selection by the USEF committee.

Athletes are chosen through a combination of competition performance and "other factors," said Trent Fairfield, spokesman for the USEF.

I CLICK BACK to the search results. My stomach starts eating itself as another link catches my eye.

Hotel heiress ends engagement

July 15, 2014

Is one of America's most eligible bachelorettes back on the market?

Page Six has learned that 24-year-old Ever Beckinsale, heiress to the multi-billion dollar Beckinsale hotel chain, has ended her engagement to 28-year-old William Covington III just three months after the couple announced their plans to wed.

Beckinsale broke?

July 30, 2014

Hotel heiress Ever Beckinsale might be nursing more than a broken heart.

Sources tell Page Six that she's also mourning a broken bank account after her father, global hotel tycoon Mitchell Beckinsale, has blocked her access to family accounts for undisclosed reasons.

Sources remain as tight-lipped about this as they were about the recent break-up between Ever and her fiancé, William Covington III, earlier this month. But the timing suggests the two incidents are connected.

"Mitchell is concerned that Ever's rash decision to end her engagement shows a lack of discipline," the source said on condition of anonymity.

The elder Beckinsale apparently gave Ever an ultimatum before she left for a horse exhibition in Ireland—give up her horsing around or lose her money.

My stomach roils at the last sentence. I look again at the date on the story. *July 30, 2014.* That would've been just a couple of days after the end of the festival. I met her on a Friday.

My brain connects the dots.

Is that why she was crying that day? Is that what she was talking about when she said she wanted to run away? Because she was sad about daddy cutting her off?

My stomach is in full revolt now. I toss the laptop aside, swing my legs off the bed, and grab my head in my hands.

I gave her my Claddagh stone. My most prized fuckin' possession. The thing my brother gave me before they took him away. *No matter what happens,* he said. *Brothers forever.*

Ah, fuck. FUCK. The floor wavers through a watery lens. She probably threw it away the minute she walked away from me. She probably laughed at me. She probably told her friends about the weird Irish bloke who gave her a useless stone.

This can't be happening.

All this time, I've justified giving it to her because, well, FUCK. Because I thought she was someone else. Someone in need. Instead, she was just a spoiled rich girl who didn't want to lose her diamonds.

It was the way she looked at me. All my life, people have looked at me like something they either scraped off their shoe or, after I started showing promise in the ring, like their ticket to fame. But not her. For a few minutes, I was just me. Someone worthy. Someone kind.

I don't believe in that love-at-first-sight shite, but that girl—she made me believe in *something*. And it had been so long since I'd believed in anything. Especially myself.

Jesus, what a fool I am. A romantic feckin' gobshite.

I sit up again and reach for my backpack. My brother's letter is still safely tucked in the front pocket. I've read it a hundred times, but I need it right now. I need to remember why I'm really here and what really matters.

Dear Paddy,

Not much to report. The food still tastes like a witch's cunt in here, and I'm down to my last smoke. They let me use a computer, though. Got to see your interview with that lass from the news. She's a fine one, yeah? You sounded smart.

They say you're still the favorite for the gold. I'm kind of a celebrity in here right now because of you. The guards even said I could get out of my cell at night to watch you on TV when you spar. Not the same as being there, and I'm sorry I fucked up so bad that

I have to miss it again. But I'll be cheering you on. You remember that, yeah?

Keep your head up. Move your feet. Win that fuckin' gold, Paddy. Make me proud. Make Ireland proud. Make Ma proud.

You're the only good thing to come out of her.

Love,

Killian

MY THROAT TIGHTENS, and I fold the letter back into the envelope.

He's only in there because he was protecting me. And who was he protecting me from? A fuckin' lying rich boy who started the whole fucking thing and was never even charged. That bastard walked away like nothing happened, because who was going to believe a couple of orphans over the son of an investment banker with more money than the bloody Queen of England?

I cried like a pussy when they took Killian away. I was seventeen, but I sobbed on my coach's shoulder as hard as the day the state ripped us from our ma when I was six-years-old.

After the sentencing, that lyin' fucking prick walked right past me and actually smiled. I lunged for him, but Billie grabbed me and threw me against the wall.

"You want to join your brother?"

I struggled against him, still too scrawny to be a match for his girth. "Let me go, Billie."

Billie shoved me harder against the wall. "So you can finish what Killian started? You got a chance, boy. Don't throw it away."

I sagged against Billie's strength. "He got away with it. My brother's in prison, and that bastard walks away!"

"There's one lesson you gotta learn, boy. The laws are different for the rich. The sooner you get that, the better off you'll be."

Laws for the rich? There are no fuckin' laws for the rich.

I return the letter to its pocket. Outside my room, the party has grown to raucous-level loud. I can't go out there. I can't face her. But, Jesus, I need air. Thankfully, my room has a door leading directly to the balcony outside. If I hide in the corner, maybe no one will notice me.

The air is heavy and thick when I walk out. The city beyond smells like the ocean, a scent that should be familiar and comforting. But this is a different scent, a different sea, and I suddenly feel adrift.

Ten floors down, the sidewalks of the athlete's village surge with life and the cacophony of languages and hyped-up emotions. Four years ago, I was one of them. I was twenty-two and a reckless dickbrain who thought being the medal favorite meant I could fuck around and still win.

I was wrong.

And for two years after that—after I threw away my shot—I lived with the unending shame of my implosion, my life on a downward spiral. But after *her*, everything changed. I was a man renewed, ready to take back what was mine. Ready to be the person I saw in her eyes in those brief, promising moments by the bay.

Now it's over.

The promise is broken, leaving an Olympic-sized hole in my chest. The idea of winning the gold has even lost some of its shine.

And maybe more than anything, *that* pisses me off.

The door slides open behind me.

I know without even looking over my shoulder who it is.

4

{EVER}

IT *IS* HIM.

The truth of it brings a wave of dizziness that forces me to hang onto the doorframe. How is this possible?

I didn't believe it at first, lying on top of him and staring into eyes so familiar they made my heart race. I thought it was just my mind playing tricks on me. A mirage borne of wishful thinking and Irish accents and irrational romantic fantasy.

What are the chances that of all the people in the world I would accidentally tackle in a bathroom at the Rio games, it would be *him*?

Even when he said, "It's you," I didn't believe it. The man from Galway had a beard. This one doesn't. The man from Galway didn't have a tattoo snaking down the length of one arm. This one does.

But staring at his strong, wide back as he leans on the balcony railing, I know it's true. It *is* him.

My emotions war with each other until uncertainty is the only one that breaks through. I have no idea what to say to him. No idea how to explain what our brief encounter two years ago meant to me. Do I admit that I looked for him afterwards? That I asked around to see if anyone knew the man with the Border Collie puppies? Do I tell him that my eyes play games with me sometimes, that I see him in crowds around the world and in my dreams at night?

Do I tell him I carry the stone in my pocket every single day?

Taking a deep breath, I slide the door shut behind me and venture farther onto the balcony. I have no idea what to say. I just know Fate brought us back together for a reason.

It's time to find out what it is.

"Padraig?"

Lorna told me his name, and it sounds exotic and beautiful on my lips. Paw-raic.

His shoulders tense as I approach. I pause. Maybe he doesn't know it's me. "C-can I join you?"

He shrugs, doesn't even look back. My steps falter. "I'm sorry about the bathroom."

"Was an accident."

His voice is gruff, angry. What's going on?

I stop just short of the railing, close enough that I can smell the masculine scent of his skin and see the pop of muscle along his jaw.

As if he's clenching his teeth.

My heart slows into a heavy, cautious thud. "Padraig, what—"

"What kind of fuckin' name is Ever?" he suddenly growls, jerking his gaze to mine.

"W-what?"

"I said—"

"I heard you," I breathe, the thud in my chest becoming painful. "You know my name?"

"Doesn't everyone know your name, sweetheart?" His voice drops, and his gaze turns lewd. "Twenty hottest Americans in Rio, yeah?"

Oh my God. I stumble back a step. "Is that—is that what you meant in the bathroom when you said, 'It's you'? You recognize me from that list?"

"How else would I know you?"

Oh my God. I am such a fool. Cheeks burning, I hug my arms across my chest as my mind races to figure out what to do. Do I tell him who I really am?

"Show jumper, yeah?" he says.

I nod, distracted, confused.

He snorts. "Figures."

"W-what do you mean?"

"That only a rich girl would choose a sport in which the fuckin' horse does all the work."

My mouth falls open, letting out a surprised whimper. I've been on the receiving end of cruel words before, but this—this feels like the jagged edge of a knife. Who is this man?

Then it hits me. The clenched jaw. The hands curled into fists. The rigid shoulders.

He's *lying*.

He *does* remember me. But at some point between the bathroom and the balcony, he learned who I am, and nothing else that happened between us before apparently matters. He took one look at my name, my background, and made up his mind about me. Just like everyone else.

My heart grows cold and heavy, like the stone in my pocket.

"Tell me, princess," he says, leaning in closer. "How did a pampered little heiress like you get to the games?"

Shock and sadness burn away with a burst of red hot rage. "Same way as everyone else. I earned a spot on the team."

"You mean your daddy's money bought you a spot, yeah?"

I snap. "Yeah. That's it. You're exactly right." I close the short distance between us until we're practically nose to nose. "Know what else I did? I fucked the entire selection committee. Because that's what worthless, spoiled, rich girls do to get their way."

I match his lewd expression from before. "You should have chased after me that day in Galway. Maybe I would have fucked you, too."

Bile burns my throat as I spin toward the door. My knees shake so badly that I'm afraid I'm not going to be able to make it. Behind me, he stumbles and lets out a short burst of air. Just as I reach for the handle to the door, I hear his voice.

"Wait."

I slowly turn. He stands a few feet away, hands on his head. His face is stripped of its hard edges, replaced by surprise and something else. Regret? Too late.

He shakes his head as if he doesn't know what to say. Then his arms drop loosely to his sides. "You *do* remember me."

"No." My voice cracks. "You are definitely not the man I remember."

Before I can humiliate myself by crying, I whip around, yank open the door, and race back inside. Every head swivels my way as I barrel through the small living room.

"Ever? Ya' all right?"

I force a smile and wave at Lorna but keep walking.

"Ever!"

His voice fills the room behind me. I pick up my pace. I grab the handle to the front door and throw it open. It crashes against the wall behind me, and I don't bother to shut it.

"Ever, wait!"

I ignore him as I jog down the hallway to the stairwell. The heavy metal door creaks as I run inside and nearly collide with a couple pressed against the wall, locked in a passionate kiss, moaning and oblivious to my intrusion.

Ducking around them, I descend the stairs in fast steps, driven only by the need to hide in my room so I can at least be alone when I lose it. As I circle the landing, my elbow bangs against the metal railing. I swear under my breath but don't stop. At least the pain in my arm is a distraction from the other pain—the one in my chest.

When will I ever learn? When will I stop being so stupid? For two years, I've wasted dreams on nothing but an illusion. A fantasy. A man who didn't care who I was or who my parents were. A man who was kind just to be kind. I might as well have pinned my hopes on a unicorn.

I should be used to reality, but I'm not.

It shouldn't feel like a loss, but it does.

His footsteps echo behind me, hard and fast, until he catches up to me on the landing for the sixth floor.

"Are you seriously going to just run away from me?"

I whip around. "What do you want? Did you forget to accuse me of destroying the European Union, maybe?"

He grimaces, managing to make it look infuriatingly sexy. "No. Just let me explain."

"No thanks. You said more than enough."

I open the door to my floor and storm through it.

"What were you crying about that day?" he demands behind me.

"None of your business."

"Because your father cut you off?"

"Jesus, will you leave me alone?"

"Ever, *please*." His hand wraps lightly around my arm from behind.

I yank free of his grip and whip around again. "Do. Not. Touch me."

He backs up, jaw clenched. "Just tell me you still have the stone I gave you. That you didn't throw it away."

Wow. That's even worse than being accused of buying my way onto the team. I shatter a little more inside as I reach into my pocket. The stone has lost its magic.

I take his hand, turn up his palm, and place the stone in the center, folding his fingers around it like he did with mine two years ago.

"I've carried this with me every day," I say. "But something tells me it's not going to have the same power it used to."

Padraig opens his fingers and stares at the stone, his expression a mixture of relief and surprise.

I turn away and make it all the way to the door to my apartment before he speaks again.

"Ever …"

I pause with my key in the door.

"I'm sorry. I shouldn't have accused you of throwing it away."

I unlock the door. "Good luck with your event."

"Ever, wait."

I walk inside.

And fall apart.

5

{PADRAIG}

SWEAT DRIPS from my forehead onto the gym floor the next morning as I sink, defeated, to a bench against the wall. My body is barely my own. I'm slow and heavy, my reactions a millisecond too late, my brain stuck in the hallway of the sixth floor.

Gnawing guilt and something that felt a lot like heartbreak kept me away most of the night. That, and a prolonged game of you-fucking-eejit-what-have-you-done.

After staring at her closed door for what felt like forever, I finally dragged my arse back upstairs, dodged Lorna's angry questions, and locked myself in my room.

I spent the next two hours reading everything I could find about her online and sadly, there was enough written about her to fill up the time—her life at some fancy prep school, her rise in the equestrian world, her various failed romances. No wonder she wanted to run away from home that day in Galway. Her entire life has been open to public consumption and, too often, ridicule.

I didn't need to know any of that that, though, to realize I'd made a huge fucking mistake last night. I figured that out in the mere two seconds it took for her to pull the stone from her pocket and place it in my palm.

She still had the stone.

In her fuckin' pocket.

Like it meant something to her.

But I never even gave her a chance. Instead, I did what I always do—jump to conclusions, let my own prejudices cloud my vision, and lash out.

I have no idea how to fix it, but I have to try.

Angry footsteps advance in my direction, and I don't have to look up to know who they belong to. Billie's hooked cadence is as familiar to me as my own.

Let the tongue-lashing begin in three ... two ... one.

"What the ever-loving fuck is wrong with you, boy?"

My coach's crusty voice echoes throughout the gym, drowning out the grunts and jabs of the other boxers sparring and training around us. Competition starts in two days, and everyone is getting in their last hard work outs before letting their muscles recover.

I'm under a microscope more than anyone else. Being the medal favorite puts a giant target on your back the instant you walk through the gates of the Olympic village, but it's Billie's arrows I'm most worried about right now.

I swipe my towel across my brow and face him head on. It's worse if you don't look him in the eye when he's giving you a much-deserved kick in the ass. "I didn't sleep well, Billie."

His crinkled cheeks suddenly sprout red stains as if someone shoved a steamer up his ass. Any day now, I'm convinced his head really is going to explode. Today might be the day.

"Oh, you didn't sleep well, did ya? Poor baby. Maybe I should make ya' a wee little bottle and tuck you in. Maybe sing ya' a sweet little lullaby, too, yeah?"

Quinn snorts a few feet away. Billie whips around. "Shut it, fuckmuppet. You're next. You think I don't know about that party you threw last night?"

Quinn drops his gaze and shuffles away. When Billie starts digging deep into the curse-word vault for gems like *fuckmuppet*, we're all in trouble.

Billie lowers his voice and bends closer to me. "You look me in the eye right now, boy, and tell me you didn't break your promise."

"I didn't break my promise, Billie."

Yet.

Billie searches my face with piercing blue eyes—the only things on his body that haven't started to deteriorate. "You want to tell me about the girl, then?"

Jesus. The man has sources that would make the Directorate of Military Intelligence sweat.

I stand. "There's nothing to tell."

"Is that right? Is that why you went chasing after her last night? Why you can barely concentrate?"

His voice dissolves into phlegmy cough that makes my chest ache just listening to it.

"She's off-limits, Paddy." He hacks a few more times and then faces me again. "You hear me? You forget about that girl and get your mind back in that ring where it belongs."

He shuffles off shouting for Quinn, as clear a dismissal as any. But I can't move. His words hold me prisoner in place.

Forget about Ever? Not possible. I may have made a promise to

Billie, but I made a promise to myself long before that—a promise to find the girl who kissed me on a wind-swept afternoon and gave me hope. If I've screwed that up, I will never forgive myself.

I grab my gear from the locker room of the training center and head out. The street is even more crowded than yesterday as hundreds of more athletes arrive and figure out where they're going. The village is a city all its own with everything we could need—cafes, bank centers, and even an emergency health clinic.

Just as I approach that, a girl walks out. She's wearing sunglasses and a USA ball cap pulled low on her brow like she's trying to disguise herself, but I would know her from a mile away. *Ever.* My feet grind to a halt as she turns in my direction. She must be headed to the equestrian center, because she has on tall black boots and a pair of form-hugging riding pants that make my mouth go dry.

She takes twenty steps toward me, unaware, but then she looks up and stops short. The movement makes the strap of her duffel bag slip down her shoulder, and she drops the paper bag in her hand.

I rush forward. "Let me help."

"I've got it," she snaps. She grabs the bag and stands, hoisting her duffel back onto her shoulder.

"Are you OK?" I ask, motioning to the health center. "I mean, are you-are you sick?"

"I have a headache."

Right. You can't pop an aspirin around here without permission. She would have to go to the health center for pain relief.

She sidesteps me. "I'm going to be late for training."

"Wait." I reach out and grasp her arm before I can talk myself out of it. She stops but, surprisingly, doesn't pull from my touch. As far as progress goes, it's weak, but I'll take anything.

"I barely slept last night, Ever."

"I'm sorry to hear that."

"All the stuff I said, I didn't mean it."

"It doesn't matter. I don't care."

The fact that she still hasn't pulled away from me suggests the opposite and gives me courage to plow on.

"Look, my arsehole of a roommate threw that party without asking me, and I was good and pissed about it."

"So you took it out on me?"

"No, that's not—" I blow out a breath and swipe my hand over my hair. "Look, it gutted me when you didn't recognize me, OK? And then Quinn told me who you were, and I just …"

Her eyes widen and she yanks from my grasp. "You just automatically assumed I was some rich snob who didn't deserve the benefit of the doubt?"

She doesn't give me a chance to answer.

"Did it occur to you that you *look different*? You had a beard then! It took me a second, OK?"

Fuck. FUCK. How could I have forgotten that? "I'm sorry, Ever. I didn't think—"

She jams her finger in my chest. "Let me make it clear to you and all the other doubters out there. I am here for one reason and one reason only. To win a gold medal. I don't care if you or anyone else thinks I deserve to be here or not, but I will not let you distract me. So there is only one thing I want from you. Stay. The hell. Away from me."

"I can't."

Her lips part, and a surprised puff of air escapes.

I grip her biceps. "I can't stay away from you. It's a miracle, us being here together like this. You have to tell me how to make this right."

Her eyes pinch in confusion. "Why do you want to?"

"Because I've thought about you every single day for you for *two years*. I scan every crowd for you. Every American accent I hear stops me in my tracks. If I've screwed up my one and only chance with you, I'll never forgive myself."

A bloke in a Portugal track suit accidentally bumps into her from the other direction, and she stumbles into my chest. I catch her with my arm around her back.

Awareness breaks in slow-motion, like a slideshow of photos fading in and out. The heat of her body. The smell of her hair. The tremble in her limbs. The lush, pink fullness of her lips as she slowly lifts her chin to stare at me.

"Give me a chance," I say in a voice that barely sounds like mine.

"Aye, what's this?" Lorna's voice suddenly breaks in behind us.

Ever's eyes go wide and round, and she jumps away from me as if we've been caught naked. I turn and glare at Lorna, who shoots me a sugary smile in return.

I know that smile. It's laced with arsenic.

"We're sort of in the middle of something here, Lorna."

"I'm not talking to you," she snaps.

I've known her for ten years and she's like a sister to me, but in the span of twenty-four hours, Ever has apparently replaced me in Lorna's priority list. Ever has that effect on people.

Ever adjusts her duffel bag again and starts to back away, apparently seeing a chance to escape.

"I'm late for training," she mumbles, cheeks red as she turns away.

I'm just about to ask her to wait when Lorna basically does it for me.

"See you tonight, yeah?" Lorna asks.

Ever looks back. "Tonight?"

"The charity ball. I saw your name on the list."

My heart takes off. "You're going to that party tonight?"

"I'm invited," Ever says. "I wasn't sure if I was going to go or not."

Lorna slugs her on the arm. "You have to go! You remember our deal, yeah?"

Lorna jerks her eyebrows a couple of times. I have no idea what they're talking about, but it coaxes a tiny smile from Ever's lips.

"OK," she says. "I'll go."

Lorna does a little dance in place. "This is going to be awesome! I'll see you later then, yeah? I'm late for practice, too."

We watch in silence as Lorna bounces away until the quiet between us borders on awkward. Finally, I sense Ever shift on her feet. Our eyes lock, and my veins vibrate with the electric shock that always races through me when she fixes those Irish-green eyes on me.

"Please," I say. "I'll do anything."

Her nod is almost imperceptible, but it eases the vise in my chest just enough to let me breathe again.

"I have to go," she says, the words barely out of her mouth before her feet carry her away.

I watch until she disappears into the crowd, and I have to fight the urge to punch the air with a victorious shout. I've been dreading that damn party more than anything else in Rio, but now it can't get here fast enough.

6

{EVER}

THE SUN HAS JUST STARTED its slow descent over the ocean by the time I'm ready for the party. A series of shuttle buses line the curb outside the athlete's condos, waiting to ferry us back and forth.

My emerald green gown slides against my legs as I walk outside. I don't normally show off my body, but I loved this dress the minute I found it in the store. The subtle curves, the strapless neckline, the beading at the waist ... I felt beautiful as soon as I tried it on.

My mother, however, had a fit when I made the mistake of telling her about it during a moment of weakness on the phone.

"It's off the rack?" she gasped.

As if buying a dress from an actual store where mere mortals might have touched it was akin to waking around in a potato sack.

I've been so nervous about this party—one more opportunity

for people to either fake an interest in me or turn their backs. But now I have another reason. *Padraig.*

My eyes immediately scan the crowd, searching for him, and I let out a breath of relief when I don't spot him. It's not that I don't want to see him. It's that I want to see him too much.

After the way he treated me last night I should feel nothing but loathing for him, but his apology this morning seemed sincere, and there was a moment when I was pressed against him that I almost forgot myself. For a moment, I was transported back two years and he was nothing but a kind stranger. The heat from his eyes sucked the air from my lungs. Those were the eyes I remembered—long black lashes that framed hooded blue pools and shimmered with unmasked desire and longing. I knew when I saw him in the bathroom that I had swum in their depths before, and the look he gave me this morning was an invitation to jump in again.

I want to jump, but I'm not a very strong swimmer. I'm terrified I'll drown.

I've been distracted all day thanks to him. I'm like a hormonal teenager—moody and sullen one minute, and all hot and bothered the next. My coach finally yanked me off the course during my practice run and asked me what the hell was wrong. I blamed my slow reactions to jet lag. I'm pretty sure he didn't buy it.

I stop on the sidewalk and glance around again.Not every athlete is invited to the party, and I still can't figure out why I'm among the Americans asked to represent the USA tonight. I hope it's because I'm considered a medal contender in my event and not because of my family name or, *ugh*, my newly minted status as certified American hottie.

But judging by the look I get from my teammate, Kate Winthrop, when she spots me, she's as convinced of my legitimacy as a party attendee as she is a member of the team. If her smile were any more forced, there'd be an actual gun to her head.

"Ah, Ever," she sneers with every ounce of old money snobbery she can muster. "I see you're still stealing spots you don't deserve."

"Nice to see you, too. Your dress is beautiful. Is that from Armani's spring collection?"

Kate ignores the compliment. "Sandra should be attending tonight, and you know it."

Sandra Boseman is a longtime friend of Kate's and, unfortunately, the woman I beat out when I was named to the team.

I force my own smile. "Can't we play nice for at least one night? I can fake it if you can."

I want to grab the words and shove them back in my mouth the minute they leave my lips, but it's too late. Her sneer practically drips with blood as she leans closer.

"Oh, darling, don't worry. The entire world will soon realize how much of a fake you are. And no amount of daddy's money is going to save you then."

She storms off in a satisfied swirl of teal chiffon, the heels of her Jimmy Choos clicking against the concrete like goose-stepping storm troopers.

You'd think I'd be used to it by now—her assertion that I don't deserve to be here. But I'm not. It stings every time to realize the woman I've idolized for years hates my guts.

Gripping my clutch a little tighter, I turn around in search of at least one friendly face.

And collide with a massive, solid chest.

Steady hands grasp my shoulders. "Careful now."

I don't have to look up to know who those hands and chest belong to. Even if I hadn't already memorized the outline of his body and the lilt of his voice, his scent alone is branded on my senses.

Like every other man milling around us, he has traded athletic gear for formal attire, but there's nothing "everyman" about the way it looks on him. His black jacket spreads tightly across impossibly broad shoulders, and I have to squeeze both hands around my purse to keep from sliding them inside to feel the muscles the jacket hides. I know they're there. I got a taste of them last night when he was naked beneath me in the bathroom.

I finally dare to look up.

"Aye," he says, smiling down at me.

I flush and back away from him. "I seem to have a bad habit of bumping into you."

He smiles. "I wouldn't call it a *bad* habit." He drops his voice. "You look beautiful."

I flush and take another step back.

He suddenly nods toward Kate, shoving his hands in his pockets. "Everything OK?"

"Fine."

"Doesn't seem fine."

I shrug. "My teammate hates me."

"Why?"

"I beat out one of her friends." A surge of defensiveness rises up before I can stop it. "You two have a lot in common, actually. She thinks I bought my way onto the team, too."

I watch the Adam's apple bob up and down in this throat. His eyes darken, and I instantly feel like a bitch.

"I'm sorry. I shouldn't have said that."

"I deserved it."

"No, you didn't."

He cocks his head, and a tiny smile takes root. "You could make it up to me."

My body goes up in flames at the mere suggestion in his tone. "How?"

"Dance with me tonight."

"Oh, I—no. I'm a horrible dancer."

"Well, I'm an excellent one, so you're covered."

He punctuates with a wink, and BOOM. My insides turn to pancake batter. And then, to make matters worse, I suddenly imagine us dancing—his arms around me, his body pressed against mine, his hand hot on my back.

His smile grows, as if he can read the direction of my thoughts. My cheeks flush like I've just been caught looking at a naughty Tumblr feed.

The door of the shuttle bus behind me slides open. Thank God. I whip around, desperate to avoid Padraig's penetrating gaze.

I drop into the first open seat I can find. Padraig doesn't wait for an invitation. He takes the open seat next to me and settles in, his wide shoulders and massive thighs taking up more than half the space. His leg presses against mine. I know it's unintentional, but my body goes up in flames all the same.

Just then, Kate walks by our seats, her nose in the air like she doesn't even notice me. I drop my gaze to my lap, hoping the disappointment doesn't show on my face.

"I know how hard that is," Padraig says, his voice low enough just for me.

I look over. "How hard what is?"

"Being misjudged for things out of your control."

The understanding in his eyes holds me prisoner.

"I've been dealing with it my whole life," he explains. "People look at me and see nothing but a roughed up loser from the wrong side of the tracks. People look at you, at your family name, and assume you're just a spoiled rich girl. I should know better, but that's exactly what I did to you last night, and I'll be sorry about that for as long as a I breathe."

My chest shifts at the heartfelt, urgent apology. No one ever apologizes. At least not with real meaning behind it.

I deflect with a shrug. "I have no right to complain about anything. My family could buy and sell entire countries."

"But all that money didn't save you from being lonely, did it?"

Lonely. The word crashes through my body and breaks things. I've spent my entire life drowning in the unwanted fish bowl that is my family—exposed and dissected at every turn—but I've never felt as bare as I do right now under the spotlight of that one word. Because no one, not until now, has ever looked deeply enough to realize I'm swimming alone.

How does he see that? How does he see *me*?

I force a laugh to cover the effect of his words. "That's why I tend to like horses better than people."

"I'd like to be the exception."

He reaches over and brushes his thumb across my bottom lip, his eyes gazing upon my mouth as if the answers to all of life's questions are on my lips. Time moves in slow-motion, because I know what's about to happen, and I want it to happen. His breathing picks up in time with mine, and I wonder if his heart is pounding as hard, too.

My lips suddenly crave his like an addict looking for a fix. My one remaining sane brain cell warns that giving in might be just as destructive as taking a hit, because Lord knows, the withdrawal will kill me. But I can't help it. I let my eyes drift closed as he lowers his head. His mint-scented breath tangles with mine. His lips hover, teasing and taunting me.

I realize in a fog what he's doing. He's going slowly to give me a chance to push him away, to say no. But just when I'm ready to say *yes*, he pulls back and instead presses his forehead to mine.

"I have dreamed about kissing you for two years," he whispers, his voice taut and tender at once. "But I'm not going to. Not until you give me a chance to earn it."

His hand snakes between us to cover mine where they're bunched against my lap. The heat of his fingers is comforting and oddly reassuring—as if there is no reason at all to be embarrassed that we're practically making out in the middle of the bus.

OMG. What. The Hell. Am I Doing? I really am almost making out in the middle of the bus. With a guy who insulted me so horribly last night that I spent the rest of the night alternating between bawling into my pillow and punching it. I have completely lost my mind. My face burns as I pull back. My eyes scan for any phones pointed in our direction, because that's just what I need—photos of me in a compromising position being leaked to the press.

I turn to stare out the window, but as soon as I do, I feel the heat of him against my back. Then his voice tickles the bare skin of my neck.

"You take my breath away," he murmurs.

So how come when the bus finally pulls away from the curb, I'm the only one struggling to breathe?

7

{PADRAIG}

I HATE PARTIES LIKE THIS—HIGH-CLASS shindigs with tiny food and massive egos. I've been bumped into, spilled on, and had my ass grabbed twice by women old enough to be my grandmother. But the worst part is that we've been here ninety minutes, and I haven't gotten Ever on the dance floor once.

The minute we arrived, she was ushered away by some Team USA media person who had lined up all kinds of interviews and photo ops for her. Ever walked away with a terrified glance over her shoulder, but the instant the cameras turned on, she morphed into someone else. Someone who has obviously spent more than her fair share in front of crowds and photographers. She morphed into the person they expect to see—a poised, beautiful woman of wealth and privilege.

Funny, though. I already know the signs of how uncomfortable she is. It's in the tight grip of her hand around her purse, the subtle pinch at the corner of her eyes, the tilt in her head when she smiles and nods.

I already know that the Ever she gives to the world is not the real her. The real Ever lashes out when she's mad but clams up when she's embarrassed. The real Ever carried that damn stone in her pocket every day for two years. The real Ever thinks she can put on a brave face and cover up the sadness lingering behind her eyes.

I will do whatever it takes to earn *that* Ever's trust. To earn the kiss that I damn near planted on her in the bus and am still feeling the dizzying effects of now.

"Wow, you're bloody pathetic, mate."

I look up just as Lorna grabs a chair at my table, turns it around, and sits down backwards. If she were any other woman, I would take the time to appreciate the way her dress hikes up her impressive legs, but this is Lorna. Besides, I'm not sure I'll ever notice anyone but Ever from now on.

"You're talking to me again?"

She shrugs. "Maybe."

She follows my gaze to where Ever is huddled politely with an older couple and a thirty-something bloke whose eyes can't seem to find its way above the creamy mounds of cleavage peeking out of her dress.

"What's up with you two?" Lorna asks.

"Nothing."

"The way you're looking at her right now is not *nothing*." She kicks my foot. "Spill."

Again, if it were anyone else, I'd tell them to mind their own feckin' business. But again, this is Lorna, and she's going to hound me until I give her what she wants.

I scrub a hand over my hair and let out a long breath. "You

remember that girl I told you about? The one I gave my Claddagh stone to?"

"Yeah. So?"

I nod toward Ever.

Lorna blinks twice in confusion. Then she jerks back. "Get out. It was Ever?"

"Crazy, no?"

"Not if you believe in fate."

"Do you?"

She shrugs. "Sure. Why not? What else is there to believe in?"

Lorna has her own demons. She doesn't talk about them much, but whenever she comes up with sage bits of advice like that, I know she's hiding something.

She suddenly shakes her head. "Wait, I don't understand. If Ever is your long, lost dream girl, what happened last night?" Her eyes get big and she groans. "No, don't tell me. You found out she's a rich girl and said something shitty."

I could explain further—how Ever didn't recognize me at first and all that shite—but even I know it doesn't excuse my behavior. "I'm not proud of it."

Lorna lays into me with a string of cuss words that would make Billie blush and finishes with a slap upside my head. I duck, but not fast enough. Jesus, but the lass is strong.

"What the hell is wrong with you, Padraig? Ever is a nice lass."

"I know—"

"And a good person. Did you know she started a summer camp for children who lost their parents at war so they can learn to ride horses?"

"Yes." I don't mention that I only know that because I Goggled her *after* laying into her last night.

"And she's smarter than both of us combined, you eejit. Did

you know she graduated from high school a year early and speaks fluent French?"

Yes. Dammit.

"She's deserves better than your fuckin' hang-ups, Paddy."

I bang my fist on the table. "I know, OK?"

"So, what are you going to do about it?"

I find Ever in the crowd again, still talking to the same people. "I'm working on it."

"Work harder."

The lead singer of the band announces they're going to slow things down as the musicians start strumming the melody of a classic Sting ballad. I look back at Ever to find her gazing at me, but she quickly looks away when our eyes meet.

Lorna's right. Enough waiting. I stand so quickly, my glass of water jostles and nearly falls over.

The prick staring at her tits notices me first. My expression must say something along the lines of I WILL FLATTEN YOU, because he literally backs up as I approach.

Ever looks over her shoulder again. "Padraig," she says, surprise adding a lilt to her voice.

I will never tire of hearing my name from her lips.

She smiles politely at the older couple. "Mr. and Mrs. Kincaid, I'd like to introduce Padraig O'Callahan. He's a boxer from Ireland and—"

I grasp her hand. "Pleasure to meet you folks, but if you'll excuse us, I promised this lass a dance tonight, and the band is playing a good one."

She tags along behind me, hand tightly clasped with mine, and lets out a little giggle which, God in heaven, makes me want to strip her naked. I take her purse from her other hand and toss it to Lorna as we pass the table.

"Hold this, will ya'?"

Lorna catches it and snorts. "Oh, sure. I'll just sit here, then."

But there's a smile in her voice when she says it, so I know she doesn't really mind.

The singer starts crooning out the words when I get Ever to the dance floor and draw her into my arms. My body reacts like a man who has just wandered out of the desert and discovered a cool pond. There's a moment of shock followed by soul-drenching relief. I want to dive in and drown.

Ever's tentative fingers fold into mine as I slide my other hand around her waist. I splay my fingers against her lower back with just enough pressure to guide her. It takes all my willpower, though, not to crush her fully against me as we start to move. She fits against my body like she was born to be there. Hell, maybe she was. Her head tucks under my chin, her body a breath's width from mine.

For the first few seconds, she's hesitant in my embrace, stiff in her motion. But then she relaxes into me with an exhale. Her hand inches farther up on my shoulder.

"You're right," she says, tilting her chin up to look at me. "You are a good dancer."

I twirl her and am rewarded with a lyrical laugh as I pull her back in, closer this time. She lets me tuck our hands against my chest, and we sway together in time to the music.

"Can I ask you something?" she asks after a moment.

I dip my mouth closer to her ear. "Anything."

"Who gave you that stone?"

My chest tightens. "My brother."

"You have a brother."

She states it as fact, not a question, as if she's filing the information away. "Older or younger?"

"Older by two years."

"Is he coming to Rio?"

"Nah, he—" *Can't make it. Is busy. Couldn't get the time off.* Plausible lies are on the tip of my tongue, but I don't want to lie. Not to her. "He's in prison."

I wait for the inevitable shock, but it doesn't come.

"What for?" she simply asks.

"He got in a fight. A man died."

Even after all these years, I can't say the word *murder*. I have a brother in prison for murder.

"I'm sorry, Padraig. That must be hard."

I slide my hand up her back to hold her closer. "Can I ask you something now?"

"Yes."

"What were you running away from that day?"

8

{EVER}

THE QUESTION WAS PREDICTABLE, and I should have been prepared for it.

I'm not.

I don't even know where to start.

"Did it have something to do with your father threatening to cut you off?"

"It's complicated."

His fingers spread wide against my back. "You don't have to tell me."

"I want to, but …"

He pulls back just enough to look down at me, and I feel the pull of his gaze like my own personal gravity.

"But you don't really trust me yet," he says.

A weird stirring in my gut sends a surge of uncharacteristic courage to my tongue. "I want you to know me. Not the girl you saw that day or the rich girl who everyone thinks bought her way onto the team. I want you to know the *real* me."

His eyes darken with a hunger that makes me shiver.

"I want to know that girl, too."

"Then I'm going to show you something."

I back away from him on the dance floor and hold out my hand. His lips tug up at the corners into a sexy smile as he links his fingers with mine. I lead him back to the table, thank Lorna for watching my purse, and then pull him behind him into the hallway outside of the ballroom.

"Where are we going?" he asks, tightening his hold on my hand.

"To meet a friend."

A shuttle is waiting outside, and I ask the driver to take us to the equestrian center. It's a short drive away, and we ride in silence in the front row of seats until we reach the building.

It's sort of against the rules, bringing him here this late. Security around the stables is among the tightest of the games because, believe it or not, horses can be targets for sabotage. But a little sweet talking in Portuguese—I'm not fluent, but I know enough from my travels—and the guard lets me bring Padraig in.

"What are we doing here," Padraig whispers close to my ear.

"I told you I want you the real me," I answer with a shrug. "This is where she lives."

His eyes get all warm and soft as he looks at me, and my whole body revs up with an unfamiliar energy as he takes a step closer.

"Show me your home, then," he murmurs.

I lead him through the wide entry hall and around a corner to the main corridor.

He looks around and barks out a surprised. "This place is nicer than the athlete condos."

"Well, the horses do all the work, so ..." I say. I smile, though, so he knows I'm kidding.

"You're never going to let me live that down, are you?"

"Not yet, at least."

We're alone as we walk down the long, wide corridor. The horses' stalls line both sides, and though most of the animals are quiet and bedded down for the night, a few greet us with a peek and a snort over their gates.

"How do they get here? The horses, I mean."

"We fly them here. There are specialized cargo planes built just for horses."

"You're shitting me. How much does that cost?"

"A lot. Which is why rich girls like me are usually the only ones who can afford this sport."

"Aye." Padraig grips my elbow and pulls me to a stop. "I only asked because I was curious, not because I was judging ya'."

"I know. And I was just being honest. This isn't a sport most people can afford. Some of these horses alone are worth a million dollars. Forget about the gear, the tack, the travel, the stables."

"Is that why you started a summer camp for disadvantaged children? So they can try the sport?"

Surprise and pride flood my veins. "How did you know about that?"

"Google."

I shrug, suddenly shy under his gaze and the knowledge he looked me up online. "Horses are special creatures. No lonely child should be denied their friendship just because of money."

Padraig holds out his hand. "Then I look forward to meeting your friend."

My stall is the last on the left. It's quiet inside, but I know he's not asleep yet. He won't settle down in a strange place until I bid him good-night.

"Hey, buddy," I croon. "I'm here."

I let go of Padraig's hand so I can open my purse. The only thing inside besides my ID, some cash, and my phone is a baggie of carrots and apple slices. The sound of crinkling plastic brings him shuffling forward. His long, brown snout peeks over the gate.

"There's my boy," I whisper. I lean forward and kiss his nose, breathing in the velvet scent of him. He snorts and nuzzles my shoulder.

Padraig whistles softly next to me. "He's huge. What do you call him?"

I point to the nameplate above the stall. *Bobby McGee.*

Padraig clears his throat. "Like the Janis Joplin song?"

I dig a carrot from the bag. "Mmm-hmm."

"Who-who named him?"

I feed an apple slice to Bobby. "I did."

"Why Bobby McGee?"

"I was there when he was born. I was fifteen and going through a sort of rebellious sixties and seventies phase. I was listening to all that music at the time—you know, Bob Dylan, The Mamas and the Papas, Simon & Garfunkel. I thought I was so profound."

I flash a peace sign at him. He cocks a one-cornered smile that gives me the feels way down in my stomach again, and then he leans back against the gate.

I feed Bobby another carrot. "Anyway, the mare was having trouble giving birth. She'd been laboring for hours, and we'd been out there with her all night. One of the stable guys suggested I sing to her because she would always come running whenever she heard my voice. He thought it might calm her down a bit. I swear, the only song I could think of on the spot was—"

"Me and Bobby McGee," Padraig says, his voice tight.

I look up again. "Yeah."

His expression is blank, but the tension in his shoulders reveals something is simmering beneath the surface.

"Are you OK?" I ask.

"Fine." He clears his throat. "Tell me more."

I study him a moment longer and then turn back to Bobby. "I started singing it, and all of a sudden, the mare gave one big push, and out he came."

I kiss Bobby's nose again. "It was the most amazing thing I'd ever seen. He was so strong. He stood almost immediately, and I just knew what his name had to be."

"Bobby McGee."

I nod, feeding Bobby the last of the apples.

"And you've been singing that song to him ever since, haven't you?"

"Every night."

Our eyes lock, and the air ignites between us. I quickly look away, afraid I'll self-combust.

"When did you start riding?"

"When I was three."

"*Three*?"

"My parents got me a pony for my birthday." I shake my head. "That sounds pretty stereotypically rich girl, doesn't it?"

"Enough of that. Tell me about the pony."

I lay my palm flat for Bobby to eat another slice of apple. "Her name was Trudy. Apparently I wanted to spend every minute with her and drove my parents crazy wanting to go over to the place where she was boarded so I could ride her. My parents finally broke down and built a stable and pasture on our estate so I could ride her every day. By the time I was ten, we had five horses and I was training every day."

"Where's your estate?"

I wince and hope it doesn't show. "Connecticut. But I don't live there anymore."

"Where do you live now?"

"Kentucky."

"Alone?"

I side-eye him, and he winks with a flirtatious smile.

"Alone," I emphasize. "Unless you count the thirty horses I'm in charge of."

"Impressive herd."

"Only ten are mine. I'm the stable manager. I had to—" I clear my throat. "I started working there after my dad kicked me out and blocked my access to the family bank account."

I sneak a glance at him. The flirtatious gleam is gone.

"Your dad kicked you out?"

"Technically, I left, but he didn't really give me much choice. If I quit riding and joined the hotel business, I could stay at the estate. If I didn't, then he'd cut me off, and I'd have to leave."

"So you ran away from home."

I nod, scratching Bobby's nose. "I wasn't crying about the money, Padraig. I was crying because part of me considered staying, and it really pissed me off to realize how weak I was."

Holy shit. I really just said that out loud. Truth bombs are exploding all around me tonight.

I suck in a breath and let it out. "Anyway, I left. I had some money left from my competition winnings, and it was enough to buy Bobby back—"

"Wait." Padraig stands tall and rigid. "He sold Bobby?"

"He sold all my horses."

"Why?"

"To punish me."

"For what?! For not wanting to spend your life working in a hotel?"

"For disobeying him. For not living my life the Beckinsale way." I drop my voice to a mocking tone. *"You have responsibilities to this family, Ever.* I didn't want to go to the college they picked for me. I didn't want to work in the hotels all my life. I didn't love the man they basically selected for me—"

"Your fiancé," he interrupts, voice rough.

I nod. "He was perfect in every way. For *them.* It took me far too long to figure that out."

"So you dumped him, moved out, and your father punished you by cutting you off and stealing your horses."

"That sums it up, yeah."

"No offense, Ever, but I don't like your parents very much."

I shrug. "They are who they are."

"How'd you get the rest of your horses back?"

"I worked out a deal with the stable where my dad sold them. I knew the owner anyway from the competition circuit. I work as his stable manager and pay him a portion of all my winnings."

And next month, when I finally get my trust fund, I can buy them all outright. I don't tell Padraig that, though. He's just getting to know the Ever-the-stable-manager and the Ever-the-athlete version of me. Judging by his reaction last night to the misconception that I was Ever-the-heiress, I'm not ready for him to know I'm about to become Ever-the-trust-fund-baby.

Besides, I still don't know why he reacted so strongly to Ever-the-heiress. Experience has taught me people's reasons for their prejudices against me often matter more than their misconceptions.

"So, what do you live on?" he asks, interrupting my thoughts.

"Ramen noodles."

I meant it to be funny, but Padraig doesn't laugh. I glance at him and find him watching me with furrowed brows and a clenched jaw.

"That was a joke. I also eat a lot of cereal."

"You gave up everything," he says.

"It was worth it."

The look he gives me is pure fire. The flames nip at my skin, dance along my nerves, heat the breath in my lungs. He stares at me like he wants to burn alive, and the unmasked desire in his expression makes me go heavy and wet. My body scorches with a need so sudden, so hot, so wild, that I can barely speak.

"Do you—" I have to pause and catch my breath. "Do you want to pet him?"

His hooded eyes darken even more. "Show me how."

"Come closer."

I hold my breath as he circles around behind me, bringing with him an intoxicating scent—a masculine cocktail of soap and skin and unbound sexuality.

"Give me your hand," I say, though how I manage to speak over the loss of oxygen in my lungs is a miracle.

Padraig takes a single step closer, enough to bring him flush against my back. I feel everything at once. The heat of his body. The brush of his arm. The tickle of his breath on my hair. The rapid gallop of my heart.

The entire world slows to a crawl as he places his hand in mine. I lift it and turn his palm against Bobby's strong, wide jaw.

"Like this," I whisper, rubbing Padraig's hand in a slow circle against Bobby's silky hide.

"He's soft," Padraig murmurs.

I nod. It's all I can do, because my vocal chords are useless. My entire existence is reduced to a single centimeter square in the center of my palm where my hand touches his.

My entire mind is reduced to a single, irrational, wild thought.

Before this night is over, I want his hands all over me.

9

{PADRAIG}

MY HANDS HAVE KNOWN pain and caused pain.

They've defeated champions with their power and strength.

They've spent most of my life balled into tight fists, first out of youthful anger and, later, out of controlled aggression.

But right now, my hands are useless under the feather-light caress of Ever's fingers.

A few stalls down, a horse whinnies softly. Another rustles against his door. They're the only sounds in the building besides our labored breathing, but I hear none of it. My senses exist for one reason—to soak in this sublime torture of being touched without touching, of trying and failing to hold at bay the images her caress creates in my mind.

She's seducing me. Making love to me with her hand. Manipulating my emotions the same way she's manipulating my palm against the horse's hide.

The pounding of my heart makes it hard to hear, but her voice breaks through. Soft. Hesitant. And sweetly off-tune.

Oh my God, she's singing.

She's singing *Me and Bobby McGee*.

I close my eyes, and suddenly I'm a child again. Lying on my mattress on the floor, shivering under a blanket, my ma running her fingers across my fevered forehead, singing softly about freedom and Bobby McGee to help me fall asleep.

It's the only untainted memory I have of her, and it's even sweeter now.

My eyelids slowly open again, and I don't care that I have a voice that could make the nuns weep. I tighten my fingers against Ever's, and I whisper the words along with her.

Our breathless, imperfect voices blend together, our own improbable harmony.

I don't want to touch the horse anymore. I want to touch her. Only her.

I trace my knuckle down the side of her arm. Ever shivers, goosebumps dotting her skin in the wake of my caress. She's pale and porcelain against the loud swirl of my tattoos.

She's soft where I'm hard.

Small where I'm big.

Perfect where I'm marred.

Ever's voice falters and her body sways into mine. I snake my free arm around her waist and press my lips close to her ear, the lyrics for her only.

She trembles against me, he breath coming faster. Above the line of her dress, her breasts rise and fall with every gulp of air.

I let my hand drift higher to her shoulder. My fingers dance across smooth sinew, defined muscles.

I didn't know until now that lips could actually ache for

someone else's, but anticipation is a potent throb as I dip my head to brush my lips across her shoulder—just a sweep across her soft skin as I inhale the scent that clings to her, the mingling tease of lavender and spice that I can't get out of my mind.

In all my life I've never been so nervous to kiss a woman, but with Ever, I'm afraid one mistake and she'll vanish. She's a skittish foal, and I've already given her reason to distrust me. If I could go back in time, I'd kiss her right there on the bathroom floor.

If I could go back in time, I'd never let her walk away from me in Galway.

With the pad of my thumb and finger, I gently grip her chin and tilt her face back toward mine.

Our noses touch.

We're barely kissing. Just hovering, nudging, open-mouthed and breathing each other in.

"Padraig," she whispers. And then she presses her lips to mine.

Oh my God. I've been with plenty of women and kissed even more of 'em, but not like this. I've never had a single kiss knock the air from my lungs and the strength from my knees. But everything about this kiss is different, because everything about this *girl* is different.

With this girl I'm not thinking of how to take it farther, how to speed up this part so I can get to the good part. With this girl, I'm only thinking of right now and how good it feels to hold her, how perfect she is in my arms, and how luscious her lips are molded against mine.

With this girl, this *is* the good part.

She's heaven and joy and sweetness. She tastes like life itself and everything good in it.

Ever makes a noise, a whimper-like sound as I plunge deeper into her mouth, my tongue breaking the seam of her lips. The whimper becomes a moan, and she suddenly twists in my arms so we're facing each other.

Her arms wind around my neck. Her fingers tangle in my hair. I'm not even thinking anymore, just acting. I back her up against the wall next to the gate and cradle her head in my hands.

Our bodies push and grind against each other, frantic and probing for something, anything, to ease the pent-up, spiking fever that threatens to burn us alive.

What was I saying about just kissing her being enough? Not even close. I need to consume her.

I feel an impatient, prickly bump and a puff of air against my cheek. Ever suddenly laughs and pulls back. Bobby nudges me again and huffs in my face.

"I think he's jealous," she whispers, reaching up to scratch his nose.

I'm panting and hard as hell, but somehow I manage to speak. "He's used to being the only man in your life, yeah?"

"The only one I sing with, at least."

I don't know why, but that statement seems important, and I feel something in my chest—a weird tightness I can't explain. It's like I've been standing on the edge of a cliff and suddenly, foolishly decide to leap.

I should be screaming, flailing, afraid of what's at the bottom, but I'm not. I just know I'm falling. Fast.

And it feels a helluva lot like flying.

10

{EVER}

I BARELY HAVE time to catch my breath before he leans down again. But this time when he kisses me, it's soft and patient, a slow burn rather than a flash fire. His lips move over mine with a sweet hesitance, as if he's suddenly unsure of himself.

I feel him swallow as his hands find anchor on my waist. "That was worth the wait."

I nod and then nearly swoon when he wraps his arms around me for a simple, warm hug. His chin rests on my head as he tucks my cheek against his chest.

"Thank you for bringing me here," he says.

"Thank you for coming with me."

He holds me a moment longer and then pulls back, gazing down at me.

"Can I take you home?"

It's a simple question on the surface, but it's layered with meaning. He's not talking about making sure I get home safely. He's not even asking me about sex. (Which, holy shit, if he is, the answer is *yes*.)

He's asking what happens next.

He's asking me if I'm ready and willing to give him a chance.

My mouth moves without prompting from my brain. It answers straight from my heart. "Yes."

His hands cup my cheeks seconds before he drops a short, gentle kiss on my lips. The sweetness of it should have been enough to cool down the inferno raging inside me, but it has the opposite effect.

I want him naked.

Now.

I quickly go through the routine of getting Bobby bedded down again before letting Padraig grab my hand and pull me back down the long corridor. Our footsteps beat a frantic beat against the concrete.

We find a shuttle at the stop outside that's just about to pull away. Padraig waves down the driver to stop. It's nearly empty when we board, except for a couple making out in the middle. Padraig grasps my hand again and pulls me to the back.

I take the seat by the window as the bus starts to pull away. Padraig sits down next to me, and an instant later the lights go out.

He makes a noise that sounds like a growl, and I'm back in his arms. Our lips collide in the dark and finally, Thank God, *finally*, I slide my hands inside his jacket. They roam over wide, solid mass of man. Beneath my palm, his heart hammers inside his chest.

His mouth wrenches from mine to kiss a path down my jaw and farther still to my collarbone. I fall back against the window and grip his head in my hands. I can't keep my moan inside as his tongue dips into the valley of my cleavage.

I'm not like this. Passionate. Out of control. Public. But I've waited two years, too, and now that my body has gotten a taste of his fire, need and desire burn me from the inside out.

I feel his hand on my leg, inching a slow journey up my leg from my knee to my thigh, drawing my dress up as he goes. I squirm with need.

He looks up suddenly through hooded, dark eyes. "Tell me where to touch you," he whispers.

"Where do you want to touch me?"

"Everywhere."

My hips rise involuntarily. "Touch me," I beg.

He claims my mouth again, and I quickly realize it's to cover the sound of my moan. He wastes no time. His hand slides up my inner thigh. He fumbles with the thin fabric of my thong and pushes it aside.

His finger slips inside me before I even have time to anticipate the pleasure. It's sudden, fierce, hot. My hands shoot out to brace against the seats as my hips meet his thrust.

I hear a groan and only belatedly realize it was from him.

"Oh my God, Ever," he breathes against my lips, his fingers pumping in and out. "Being inside you is going to feel like heaven."

It already feels like heaven to me.

His thumb finds the sensitive nub in the center of me and circles it gently.

My eyes slide close, but he whispers against my lips. "Don't look away. Look at me."

Our eyes lock, and what I see in his makes my chest swell with an emotion I don't understand. An emotion I've never felt before. What we're doing is erotic and borderline indecent, but the tenderness in his gaze makes it feel intimate, loving. I've always been shy about sex, but the thought of staring at him as I ....

Oh God. Every thought escapes my mind as I feel the stirrings of an explosion. The sounds of the other couple in the middle of the bus are an aphrodisiac. I don't know what they're doing, but they're enjoying it, and I feel like a cheap porn addict for admitting it, but dear God, it turns me on.

"Padraig," I pant, my hips moving of their own volition. "Don't stop. Please."

He kisses me again, his tongue pumping in and out of my mouth in time with his fingers.

It hits me suddenly. A thousand waves of light and pleasure shoot through my limbs, and my most intimate muscles spasm around his fingers. I clench my thighs together and hold in my cry, clutching his arm so hard I probably leave a bruise.

His kiss swallows the sounds of my orgasm even as he strokes every last tremor from my body until I slump against the seat, boneless. I come back to myself in pieces—the gentle rocking of the bus, the cool glass behind my head, the hot press of his hand against me, the tender nuzzle of his nose against my neck.

Holy shit. I just had the most amazing orgasm of my life on a bus. And the only thing I can think to do is cover my face with my hand and laugh.

"I can't believe we just did that."

He chuckles and gathers me in his arms. He scoops me up like a doll onto his lap, his lips pressed against my temple. I bury my face in his neck, breathe in the scent of sweat and desire. I should be embarrassed or maybe even ashamed, but I don't. I feel nothing but safe and adored in his arms, like this is where I'm meant to be.

"That was amazing," I finally whisper.

"We have two years to make up for, Ever. We're just getting started."

11

{PADRAIG}

WE BARELY GET the door closed to her apartment before we're on each other again. Her purse falls to the floor as I back her against the wall. I brace my hands on either side of her face and mold my mouth to hers. Jesus, I could kiss this woman forever.

Ever's hand slides along my jaw until her fingers tangle with the hair at the base of my neck. I burn everywhere she touches. It's as if she's found my *on* switch. I'm no longer in control of my body or my thoughts. Every motion, every action—driven by the singular need to quench a thirst that started two years ago.

Her bedroom is just off the living room down a short hallway. I sweep her into my arms and carry her there, setting her down gently inside.

"Turn around," I order.

She spins in my arms and presses her hands to the wall next to her bed. Ah, God. Even the back of her neck drives me crazy. I brush her hair aside and press my lips there. She sucks in a breath and tilts her head to give me greater access. I take it. I taste her, tracing my tongue from to her earlobe.

"You smell so good, Ever."

I draw down her zipper, inch by inch, exposing her skin to my touch, my lips, until it falls in a green pool at her feet. The sight of her body brings me to my knees behind her. I'm a lost man in a dark tunnel, and she is the light. The way out. The way home.

Gripping her hips, I skim my lips across the perfectly rounded mounds of her chiseled glutes. She moans, whimpers, and arches into me, so I do it again. I nip, suck, bite until her legs shake and she begs for more.

I turn her in my hands, still kneeling before her. Worshipping her. I'm at her mercy, and I don't even mind. As my hands slip the shoes from her feet, I press my lips to the wet strip of lace covering her sex. With an almost tortured moan, she tangles her fingers in my hair and holds my head.

She's killing me. She's feckin' killing me with her moans and her unabashed passion.

I stand and give her a playful shove. "Lie down."

She laughs and falls back on the bed while I shed my clothes as fast as I can. I yank the loose bow tie from my collar and throw it before letting my jacket fall to the floor. I attack the buttons of my shirt next, but my fingers shake so bad I can barely hang onto them. Ever rises to her knees to help. With every button she opens, she presses her lips to my exposed skin, and Holy shite, it's a miracle I don't explode in my pants.

"We are officially living out every fantasy I've had for the past two years," I groan.

She laughs again—God, how I love the sound of her laugh— and pushes the shirt from my shoulders.

Shoes. Pants. Boxer briefs. I strip as fast as I can, which isn't fast enough, because holy fuck, Ever is reclined on the bed waiting for me with her fingers hooked in the waist of her panties.

Wait. Condom.

I dig through my discarded pants and dig out one of the rubbers I put in my wallet before the party. Then I crawl onto the bed, covering her body with mine. Skin to skin, our moans mingle inside her mouth at the pleasure of my hard, probing length settling between her legs. The desire to be inside her is a physical ache, an emotional urgency.

She wiggles out of her panties beneath me. I roll us both until she's on top because I want to see her. I want to watch her eyes as I enter her. I want to hold her, guide her back to that place where she was panting my name and coming apart in my arms.

I scoot to sit up against the headboard as she straddles me. I quickly sheath myself in the condom while she braces her hands on my shoulders.

I'm shaking with need. Holy fuck … I need her now.

And then finally, thank God, she slides down on my erection.

She immediately arches back with a moan, driving me deeper inside her. Her body welcomes me into her tight, wet heat like our bodies were meant to be joined. Willpower is the only thing that stops me from emptying myself in her right then and there.

My hands find the clasp of her bra and fling it off her before filling my greedy hands with her breasts. She bends into my touch until our foreheads brush. Her hips undulate against me, pumping, pushing, and pulling toward the release we both need.

I grip her face and kiss her. Hard. Deep. Pouring into her every emotion I feel but can't find the words to say. Nothing is adequate. Words are useless. How do I explain something to her that I can't understand myself?

She's whimpering, grinding against me. I grip her hips and guide her.

"Ride me, Ever," I whisper, wrenching my mouth away. "Take what you need from me. Take your pleasure."

Faster. Harder. She pumps her hips, and I rise to meet every thrust.

Her fingers dig into my shoulders.

My teeth graze her nipples.

She lets out a cry.

And explodes.

She clenches and pulses around me with an intensity that sends me over the edge with her. Spasms of primal pleasure tear a guttural grunt from my lungs, and all I can do is cling to her as we ride it out together.

Her sweat-soaked torso slides against mine as she collapses in my arms, panting, limp, and pliant. If I had any functioning brain cells, I would say something profound or romantic, but I got nothin'.

Instead, I tuck her head against my shoulder and slide my hand up her spine until my fingers meet the long cords of her neck. When my thumb traces a slow circle beneath her ear, I'm rewarded with a soft purr of pleasure from deep in her chest.

"Like that?" I murmur.

"Mmm hmmm." She burrows her face deeper into my neck. "I'm never touched like this."

I have no idea what she's talking about. She's not a virgin, so I know she doesn't mean sex. "How am I touchin' you?"

"Like it means something to you."

It does. More than I should probably admit yet if I don't want to scare her off.

I turn my head to nuzzle her hair. "You were born to be touched like this, love."

I don't know why, but my words make her go still against me. Even her chest ceases its slow rise and fall against mine. I roll us together until she's on her back and I'm hovering over her. She immediately turns her face toward the wall, but not before I catch sight of a tear slipping across the bridge of her nose.

"Hey now, what's this?"

She rolls her eyes. "Nothing."

"Talk to me."

"That was just a nice thing you said, that's all."

Christ on crutches. What kind of losers has she had in her life if something as simple as being told she deserves to be touched sends her straight to tears? I might've asked the question out loud if the fear of her answer didn't make the growing ache in my chest even worse. So, I do the only other thing I can think of to make her tears stop flowing and my heart stop hurting.

I kiss her.

Maybe I can convey with my lips what I can't with my voice.

Maybe a kiss is enough to say, *Now that I've found you, I'm never letting go.*

12

{EVER}

HE'S STILL INSIDE ME, kissing me like he never intends to leave, and I don't want him to. He has branded me with his words, his hands, his body and soul.

His mouth lifts from mine. "I can't stop touching you, Ever," he whispers.

"I don't want you to."

He kisses me again with an urgency that quickly has me writhing and grinding against him.

He shifts his hips once, twice. I wrap my legs around his waist.

He wrenches his mouth away and presses it to my ear. "God, baby," he moans, reverence coloring his voice. "Can you come again?"

I answer with my hips. Yes. I can come again. Holy shit.

Padraig withdraws from my body, his hand hanging on to the condom. Before I have time to protest, he slides down my torso and settles his head between my legs. The first touch of his lips on my folds sends me arching again into the mattress. His tongue separates me, loves me, slowly and languidly as if we have all the time in the world.

Maybe we do. Maybe time stops in this cocoon we've made, so I tilt my head back and let him worship me again. That's what it feels like. Like being worshiped.

But patience becomes passion, and my body takes over. I pump my hips against him as he finds a steady rhythm. I grip his head and wrench out a cry as the world explodes in a riot of color and sensation. And still he doesn't stop. He loves my flesh until I float back to Earth and I'm limp against the bed.

He blows on my fevered skin and then places sweet, tiny kisses to the inside of each of my thighs.

"Be right back," he whispers. "Don't move."

His footsteps pad softly across the carpet until I hear him enter the bathroom, and that's when my ever-present friend named Insecurity comes for a visit. OMG I CAN'T BELIEVE I TEARED UP. Old voices start yelling in my head. My fiancé's. My parents. All of them telling me I feel too much. I'm too needy. Too impractical.

I force my muscles to work again to haul myself off the bed. His shirt is in a ball on the floor, so I grab it and shrug it on. I pass the bathroom and the sounds of him cleaning up.

The kitchen is just a handful of steps through the living room. I open the fridge and—

"Aye, I thought I told you not to move."

I shut the door with my hip and hold up two bottles of water, searching his face for any sign I weirded him out. There isn't any.

"Want one?"

"Sure," he says, full of swagger and sexuality as he saunters toward me wearing nothing but his boxer briefs. "I find myself rather depleted of fluids."

I shake my head. "Men."

He laughs as I throw one of the bottles at him. He catches it effortlessly with a wink. He twists off the top and downs half the bottle in the short amount of time it takes him to cross the room to me. Then he backs me up to the counter and blocks me in with his arms.

"You're looking pretty good in my shirt."

"It was the first thing I could find."

His lips land on mine, and one soul-shaking kiss later he stands. "Feel free to wear it anytime."

He starts opening cupboards above my head.

"What are you doing?"

"Since we're in the kitchen, what do you have to eat?"

"Not much, I'm afraid. My food game isn't exactly on point yet. But I do have … " I turn around and open a drawer, grab my bag of favorite candy, and spin back around. "These."

He crinkles his nose. "What are those?"

"Don't they have Twizzlers in Ireland?"

"Nah. Gimme one though. I'm starving." He jerks his eyebrows. "All that exertion, you know."

I hand over a piece and watch him devour half a vine in a single bite. He chews once and suddenly fake gags, hand over his mouth.

"What the hell is this?"

I laugh and grab the remaining candy from his hand. "It's the best candy in the world."

"It tastes like wax."

"*Strawberry* wax, thank you very much. They're my guilty pleasure."

He jerks his eyebrows again. "How about you get rid of those and let me be your guilty pleasure?"

I cock my head and look back and forth between the bag of candy and him. "I don't know. I'm in a pretty longstanding relationship with Twizzlers."

He lunges and attacks my neck with his lips. "Can they make you come three times in one night?"

"So arrogant."

"But true."

His hands sneak inside my shirt, and just when I'm getting hot again, he jumps back and steals the Twizzlers.

"These are rubbish, but I'm starving."

"Hey!" I leap for them, but he holds them aloft. "You don't get to insult my candy and then eat it."

He shoves one end of a vine in his mouth and leans toward me. I mouth the other end, and we chew toward each other until our lips touch. He winks, and boom, my insides turn to batter.

"Wanna check out the view?" he asks, nodding toward the balcony.

"We're practically naked."

"So is everyone else on their balconies."

"Have some experience with that, do you?"

"Not me." He jerks his eyebrows a couple of times and kisses me. "There's never been any other woman but you."

"Wow. Really? You're pretty good at it for a virgin."

"You think I'm good at it?"

I roll my eyes. "Fishing for compliments is beneath you."

"I just want to hear you acknowledge *three times*."

"How about you just shut up and make it four?"

Padraig lets out a growl, grabs me around the waist, and throws me over his shoulder. I shriek as he starts to run toward the bedroom.

"You're insane," I laugh.

"It's your fault."

He bends, deposits me on the bed, and immediately covers me with his body. His kiss is hungry, his touch scorching.

No one has ever been like this with me before. Strong, but tender. Demanding, but respectful. Rough, but restrained. He owns my body, does what he wants, and I let him, because I want it.

I want it when rips open the shirt and sends two buttons flying, when his teeth scrape my nipples, when he directs my hand to the waistband of his boxer briefs and begs me to touch him.

I want it when he pumps without holding back into my fist, when he rises on his knees with a growl, wraps his arm around my waist and rolls me over. I want it when he hoists my ass in the air and bends to whisper hot, dirty things in my ear about all the ways he's going to make me come tonight.

I want it when he enters me from behind, when he reaches around and rubs me where I need it until I'm nothing but a mass of wild abandon and primitive need, totally at the mercy of his body and the frantic pounding of his hips.

And when I finally come apart with Number Four, when his name erupts from my lips over and over, when he follows with a shuddering thrust and a shout, and when he collapses on my back, my name a reverent whisper on his hips, I want it all.

Because I want him.

My mystery man of Ireland.

My Padraig.

The only him I'm ever going to want again.

13

{EVER}

I AWAKEN SLOWLY with snippets of awareness.

The morning sun bathing us in warmth.

His lips on my shoulder.

The hard length of him pressing into my back.

The glide of his hand down my stomach toward the swelling pressure between my legs.

I moan quietly, eyes still closed, lost in that suspended state between sleep and arousal.

"Mornin'," he murmurs, his accent more pronounced in the heavy weight of sleepiness.

"Mmm," I respond, too lost in his touch for real words. My body aches in the most delicious way after our many rounds of lovemaking last night, but one touch from him and I already want him again this morning.

His fingers toy with the curls at the juncture of my thighs.

Teasing me. Making me wet and heavy. Making me moan with need.

"I will never get tired of the noises you make when I touch you," he says.

Then his fingers dive between my folds and enter me. I cry out and immediately cover his hand with mine, urging him deeper, pumping my hips against him.

His cock slides between my thighs from behind, slipping back and forth against my opening, teasing me.

"I want to take you like this," he groans, pumping faster with this fingers. "On your side."

"Yes," I moan, spreading my legs wider, hooking one back to give him access.

He thrusts inside me, replacing his fingers with his cock. He's already wearing a condom. He must have put one on while taunting me awake.

His hand slides up my torso until he finds my breast, kneads it, palms my nipple, all the while gliding in and out of me, tender and slow.

"God, Ever," he groans. "I could live inside you forever."

I want him inside me forever.

Number seven hits me suddenly, and he's not far behind. He leaves me to get rid of the condom, and I doze again while he's gone. But he wakes me up when he climbs back into bed and pulls me to his chest.

I rise and fall with his deep, labored breaths. Beneath my ear, his heart hammers like drum roll. I love that I can do that to him.

"This is a good way to wake up," I murmur, dropping a kiss to his perfect pecs.

He responds with a distracted mm-hmm and a squeeze of my butt cheek.

"I wish we could stay in bed all day."

"I like the way you think."

"What do you have to do today? Besides the Opening Ceremony, I mean."

"Run. Train. *You.*"

I laugh and burrow into his arms. He immediately cups the back of my head and presses his lips to the top of my hair.

"Can I come over after the ceremony?"

The shyness in his voice makes my heart squeeze. "You better."

My eyes stray to the hard swirl of colors descending down his arm. "You didn't have this tattoo before," I say, letting my fingers track the lines of the elaborate design.

"I got it a few months ago."

"Does it mean anything?"

"Lots of things."

I lean closer. He's right. It's not one tattoo but a series of vignettes connected by color. The more I study it, the more I see—vignettes and scenes from his life.

High on his forearm is an abstract woman's face. She's looking down, her face shaded.

"Who is this," I ask, rubbing my thumb over the image.

"My ma."

"She's pretty."

"Yes, she was."

I look up again at the word *was.*

He tucks a lock of hair behind my ear and answers my unspoken question. "She died when I was eleven."

Shame heats my skin. "I'm so sorry, Padraig. I didn't know. I should have asked you about her last night when you mentioned the song."

He pulls me down for a kiss. "I kept you a little busy last night."

I let him comfort my lips with his. Then he releases me and lowers his head again to the pillow.

"What happened?"

"Overdose."

I cover his heart with my hand as my shame grows. I talked about nothing but myself last night. "Padraig, I'm so sorry."

He shrugs. "I hadn't seen her since I was six anyway."

"Why?"

"We were taken away from her, my brother and me."

I want to know more, but I'm afraid to ask. "We don't have to talk about this."

"I want you to know."

I look again at the tattoo. "Why were you taken away from her?"

"She was messed up with drugs, bad people. She disappeared for a full week that summer. Left us with nothing to eat. A neighbor called child welfare to check on us after she saw my brother raiding her trash for our dinner. We'd been eating it all week."

Tears sting my eyes as my heart cracks open. My mind pictures him as a small child, starving, eating garbage that his older brother found for him. I can't help it. A tear slips down my cheek.

He smiles that soft way again and reaches up to brush away the tear with his thumb. "Hey, now," he whispers. "None of that."

"What about your father?"

"I never knew him. He ran off after I was born."

"So you were raised by a foster family?"

He tucks an arm behind his head. "Several of 'em. My brother and I were kind of a handful, so we got shipped around a lot until I was twelve. That's when Billie and Colleen took me in."

"Billie, your coach?"

"He's the reason I started boxing. He caught me fightin' one day in the alley across the street from his club. I was always getting into trouble. He jumped in and grabbed me by the collar and threw me in the ring. Told me that if I wanted to use my fists so bad, I might as well learn how to do it right. Turns out I was pretty good at it. I eventually moved in with him and his wife. He's like a father to me."

I close my eyes, shame once again heating my skin. "I'm sorry, Padraig. You must think I really am a pampered princess, complaining about my parents taking my stupid horses."

"Stop."

His hand cups my cheek. I open my eyes, and the look in his sends a healing heat through my chest.

"It's not a contest about who had the shittiest childhood, Ever. We've both been let down by our parents and forced to make our own way. We're more alike than we are different."

His words send a confusing blend of warmth and fear through me.

We're more alike than we are different. That's what I want. For him to see me as so much more than Ever the heiress. I took him to the stables last night and told him about my parents so he could see we have more in common than not.

But what about when he finds out about my trust fund?

"You OK?" he asks, brushing his thumb across my lip.

I force a smile and nod before bending to kiss him. "Just wondering how many hours I have to wait for number eight."

14

{PADRAIG}

I'VE BEEN LOOKING FORWARD to this Opening Ceremony ever since I left London with a vow I'd be back. It's one more chance to walk with my fellow Irish athletes, wave the tricolour, and represent my country and a sport I love.

I can't wait for it to fucking be over.

Just wondering how many hours I have to wait for number eight.

I check the time on my phone. The ceremony started a half hour ago, and we're barely made it through England. Half my teammates are already wasted and leanin' on each other.

I can't wait any longer. The Americans are all the way in the back, fer fuck's sake. At this rate, it'll be two o'clock in the fuckin' morning before I can crawl back into Ever's arms.

I smother a growl and pull my phone back out. I hammer out a text before I can talk myself out of it.

Meet me by the service entrance. And don't laugh.

She responds with a series of question marks and then, *On my way.*

I duck away from my country's holding station, ignore Lorna calling my name, and start jogging toward the service entrance. It's as crowded in here as free pint night at the pub. I have to push and shout my way through throngs of athletes and staffers.

She's already there when I skid around the corner. Holy fuck and thank God for American designers. The U.S. women are wearing white tennis dresses that stop at the mid-thigh. Sexism has never been so appreciated.

She takes one look at me though and bursts out laughing.

I growl playfully and yank her against me. "I said no laughing."

"I'm sorry. Really. But…"

"I look like a fucking deranged leprechaun."

She nods. "Sorry, but yes."

She's right. The Irish uniform is a disaster—green shorts, white Oxford shirts, orange suspenders, and plaid bowties.

She bites my lip and jerks her eyebrows. "You make it look good though."

Boom. I'm hard as a rock. I grab her ass. "Yeah?"

"Come on," she rolls her eyes. "You know you have the best body in the world."

"I know I've worked hard." I nuzzle her earlobe. "But a bloke still likes to hear he looks good to his girl."

Her breath catches and she goes still in my arms.

"Aye." I look down at her. "You've gone quiet."

She swallows hard and bites her lip.

"You do that, you know? You get quiet when you want to say something but you're afraid to."

Her eyes shoot up to mine like she can't believe I've figured that out.

I glance around our surroundings. Olympics staffers and security scurry about, barely paying us a glance. I spot a maintenance room fifty feet away.

"Come on," I say, taking her hand and pulling her along.

"Where're we going?"

I glance around, try the handle, and nearly shout in victory when the door opens. I tug her inside and quickly shut the door. It's a maintenance closet about the size of the bathroom in the athlete's condos.

I back her against the door and tilt her face up with my finger under her chin. The flash of uncertainty in her eyes is like a pinprick in my chest.

"Say what you want to say, Ever."

"You called me your girl," she blurts. "I'm afraid words like that mean more to me than you."

I back up and whip off my suspenders. Then I yank open my bowtie and attack the buttons of my shirt.

Her eyebrows shoot up. "Not that I'm complaining, but what are you doing?"

"Showing you what those words mean to me."

I slip my shirt off my shoulders and turn so she's staring at my tattoo. "What do you see?"

"What am I supposed to be seeing?"

"Look closer."

Her eyes search my skin and then zero in on one scene on my shoulder. Her lips part. A gasp escapes. And her fingers brush over the scene she missed this morning.

The image is an abstract picture of a woman with long dark hair staring at the water, cradled within a faded Claddagh symbol.

Her eyes waver with a sheen of wetness when she looks up at me.

"You got a tattoo of me?"

"That day was important to me, Ever. *You* are important to me."

She flattens her palm against his chest. Warmth spreads through my entire body.

"Maybe we should talk about what's happening here," I say, swallowing against a surge of that same weird emotion I felt last night. "Maybe I need to make it clear to you that I've never felt anything like it, and I'm not just talking about the physical part, which, by the way, is fucking amazing."

I reach up and move her hand to center over my heart. "I'm talking about in here. I've never felt anything like it *in here*."

Her bottom lip trembles.

"There's been no one else since the minute you walked away from me that day. You've been my girl for two years, Ever Beckinsale."

I don't know who moves first, but it doesn't matter. Our lips collide, our bodies grind against each other, our frantic breaths mingle in my mouth.

"Fuck, I missed you," I groan. "I missed you when I didn't even know you."

"I missed you, too." She sucks my bottom lip between her teeth and tugs. "I *needed* you."

It's all I need to hear. I hoist her into my arms and turn to set her on the thin strip of counter surrounding a sink against the wall. We're trembling in each other's arms, and if I could talk, I'd put a voice to the surge of emotions racing through my veins.

But I can't talk, because I'm struggling. Struggling for control, for air, for balance. Struggling with a striking uncertainty. Does she feel what I'm feeling, as if something big is happening that has nothing to do with the wild, amplified, sexed-up stakes of the games?

I grasp the zipper that runs down the front of her tennis dress and draw it down to her navel. Her breasts are hidden behind twin cups of simple white lace. I shove them aside and replace them with my hands, my mouth.

She moans and tilts her head back. "Please, God, tell me you have a condom with you."

I stand and fumble to dig my wallet from my back pocket. I nearly drop it trying to dig out the condom in the fold. I press it into her hands and then fight with the snap and zipper of my shorts. My cock springs forth, and Ever immediately wraps her hand around me.

She strokes me, staring at my face, and I wonder what she sees. Can she see what she does to me? Can she see inside where my heart beats faster and faster for her?

Her thumb suddenly circles the tip, and I almost explode right then. I groan and drop my head to her shoulder. "Put that thing on me, baby, or I'm going to come in your hand."

She does as I order and then spreads her legs wide to welcome me. I reach between us, shove her underwear aside, and thrust into her with a primal grunt.

We move with a frantic, animalistic urgency. Her nails dig into my unyielding flesh. My hands dig into her hips. I feel my orgasm build almost immediately, and I hold nothing back seeking and giving the pleasure I've only ever known with her.

Next to my ear, her pants become rhythmic pleas for more, and I feel a surge of tenderness and power. I do this to her. *I* drive her crazy.

She climaxes with a sudden, wrenching cry, and I'm done for. I follow immediately, shuddering and shouting her name. Satisfaction makes her limbs weak, and she collapses forward against my chest.

I circle her body with my arms and cup the back of her head to anchor her there.

Thoughts escape me, save one.

This is what it feels like to fall in love.

I should be terrified of the thought. I'm not.

"Padraig..."

She cups my face and forces my gaze down to hers.

"I looked for you, too," she whispers. "I flew back to Galway twice."

It takes me a minute to understand. But when it hits me, my throat gets thick. "You came back?"

"I *thought about you* every single day, too. But no one had any idea who the man was walking the Border Collie puppies. I asked everyone. *Everyone.*"

Her voice breaks on the last part, and I crush my mouth to hers. She looked for me. *She looked for me.* I don't know if I should scream over lost time or throw my hands in the air like Rocky at the top of the stairs.

We kiss with our entire souls, making up for lost time.

"God, Ever," I finally moan, wrenching away. "I never should have let you walk away that day."

"I *looked* for you. I tried."

"It's OK now," I soothe against her lips. "Because you found me."

15

{PADRAIG}

I SPEND the night after the Opening Ceremony.

The next night, I bring a bag of my stuff so I can just shower at her place the next morning rather than endure another round of Quinn's ribbing when I walk-of-shame back to our apartment.

By the fifth night, I have a key to the apartment, most of my stuff is in her bathroom and her closet, and she's adopted my favorite t-shirt for sleeping. Not that we do much of it.

By day six, I know that she sometimes murmurs hot little things in French in her sleep, shrieks when I surprise her with a kiss on the neck, and that she hates the movie The Notebook. I know she snorts when she laughs really hard, that getting her to laugh really hard is my new ambition in life, and that she is ticklish in interesting places, which makes it easier.

By the end of the seventh day, the Twizzlers grow on me, and she starts hiding them.

On the tenth day, I attend the show jumping qualifying rounds and suddenly understand perfection. I have never seen a more magical harmony than Ever and that horse. I want to pound every arsehole in the face who ever suggested she doesn't belong here. Myself, included.

The next day, I know I can't put off talking to Billie any longer, because tonight, I'm going to talk to Ever about what we're going to do when the games are over.

The gym vibrates with the boom of music from the overhead speakers and the thud of fists against bags and bodies. I finish my last training round and hover by the line of cubbies and benches along the wall to wait for him while he yells at Quinn for something.

After a few agonizing minutes that gives my brain enough time to imagine all the ways he's going to kick my ass, Billie finally turns and limps toward me.

"I need to talk to you," I say, wiping a towel down my face.

He pins me with his ice-blue stare. "Wondered when we'd get around to this."

Don't look way. Don't look away. "So you know?"

"That you ignored my advice and broke your promise?"

"It's different this time, Billie."

He hacks into his fist. "How so?"

Last time I self-destructed. This time I'm in love. "I have feelings for her."

"After a week?" he snorts.

"How long did it take for you and Colleen?"

Billie studies my face in that way of his that makes me feel like a specimen under a microscope. I brace for him to explode at me, but instead he sinks to the bench with a long, haggard sigh.

"I love you like a son, Padraig. You know that, right?"

As Irishmen, we're genetically predisposed to say, "Love you, mate," on the regular, especially when we're sloppy and leaning on each other after a few pints. But the way he says it now, using my full name like that, gives me pause.

"I know—"

"I've held you up so many times, boy. I've seen ya' kicked down by the world a hundred times and come back swingin', but something changed after London. Whether you win the gold this time or not, what's going to happen when this doesn't work out?"

"It *is* going to work out."

"Really? How? You going to fly back and forth? Tag along on her horse trips?"

"I don't know," I finally say, starting to squirm. "We've haven't talked about it yet."

"What exactly have ya' talked about then? I mean, how much do you really know about this girl?"

"I know everything that matters."

"You've never been naïve before, Paddy. Why the hell are you startin' now? You're Irish. She's American, not to mention the bloody heiress to the bloody fuckin' Beckinsale fortune."

I glare. "And I'm just a no-good orphan with nothing going for him but his fists, yeah?"

Billie stands, somber. "That's not what I was going to say at all, son, because that's not how I see you. That's how you see *yourself*. And *that's* what worries me."

I turn around and rough my hands over my hair.

"Look, son. No matter what happens, I'll always be there for you. Ya' know that. But I also know I can't stand to see ya' get your heart broken again by the world."

His hand pats my shoulder as he walks past me. I watch him

limp away, oddly unsettled because I expected worse. I wasn't prepared for the serious, quiet version of Billie.

I expected the explosion.

My phone buzzes in my pocket. I dig it out and swipe the screen to find a photo in my new messages. It's a selfie of Ever and Bobby McGee. She's kissing his jaw, and he has an Ireland hat perched on his head.

I bark out a weak laugh, covering my mouth with my hand. I told Billie I have feelings for this girl, but that doesn't even come close. I love her.

Fer fucks' sake, I even love that horse.

Hey, I finally answer.

She immediately types a response. *Everything OK?*

Good. Just got done. Catching my breath.

Thank you for going with me tonight.

Wouldn't miss it.

See you in a little while?

On my way.

I hear the shower running when I get there and find the bathroom door open. I strip off my clothes and climb in. "If you haven't gotten to your boobs yet, I get to do it."

She laughs and looks over her shoulder. "I hoped you'd get home in time to join me."

Home.

One word.

Four letters.

It packs a punch I'm not prepared for.

A feeling washes over me that transcends physical or sexual. I wrap my arms around her from behind and press my face to her shoulder.

"What's this for?" She murmurs, leaning back against my chest.

"Just wanted to hold you for a second." What the fuck is wrong with my voice?

"Mmmm…," she murmurs, covering my arms with hers. "I wish we had more time."

I know what she means—more time before we have to leave for dinner. But with Billie's words still ringing in my ears, my brain hears something different.

More time.

We only have ten days left in Rio. Do I even want to wait until after dinner to talk about our post-game plans?

She's usually the one who clams up when she has something important to say, but now it's my turn. "Ever …"

"Hmmm?"

I don't want this to end. What are we going to do when the games are over? I'm in love with you. My voice betrays me. I can't say any of them.

I turn her in my arms. Her hair is wet and slicked back from her makeup-free face. Her freckles are more pronounced in the light of the bathroom, and I trace their path with my thumbs.

"What's wrong?" she asks.

"I—nothing."

I kiss her instead and let my hands roam her wet body. Beneath my fingers, her nipples pebble and harden, and she leans into my touch. But just as quickly, she pulls back with a frustrated groan.

"We don't have time."

Time. There's that word again, haunting me. I set her back with my hands on her waist and force a smile. "Something to look forward to when we get home then, yeah?"

She rises on tiptoe and kisses me sweetly. "Definitely."

After showering, I dress quickly in my suit and wait for her in the living room. When she finally emerges from the bedroom a half hour later, she steals my breath. Will there ever come a time when I don't want to drop to my knees at the sight of her? She wears a simple black dress that hugs all the good parts and shows off toned limbs that I can't wait to have wrapped around me again. Her hair is twisted up off her neck, and I have no idea how I'm going to get through the night without putting my lips there.

"Ready?" she asks, fiddling with an earring.

I clear my throat. "Ready."

Her smile is tight. "Good. The car should be waiting for us."

I take her hand as we walk down the hallway to the lift, and that's when I feel it—a tremble in her fingers, a tightness in her muscles. She's not just nervous about tonight. She's terrified.

How much do you really know about this girl?

I have a feeling I'm about to find out.

16

{EVER}

I CAN DO THIS.

With Padraig by my side, I can face my parents.

I cling to the thought as we climb into the car waiting for us by the curb outside. His hand on my back is a warm, strong presence, like the Claddagh stone once was.

"Babe," he murmurs as the car pulls away.

"What?" I look up at him next to him.

"You're squeezing my hand so hard, I don't know if I'm going to be able to fight tomorrow."

I look at down at where our hands are joined on his leg. My knuckles are practically white from gripping so hard.

"Sorry." I ease up. "I just want to get this over with tonight."

Padraig lets go of my hand so he can wrap his arm around my shoulders. He tugs me against his side and presses his lips to the top of my head. The gesture comes so naturally to him. Sometimes he touches me without even thinking about it, as if his hands simply need to feel me. Like that hug in the shower.

He probably has no idea that his small caresses, gentle squeezes, and warm hugs are a revelation to me. He couldn't possibly know that after a lifetime of being held at arm's length by everyone who's supposed to care about me, the warm strength of his easy embraces feels like a home I've never known.

He could have no way of knowing how much it scares me because I'm already addicted to it.

I know it's not rational, what I feel for him. I'm too emotional, too sentimental. I've been hearing it all my life. It's probably not even possible to feel this way after such a short amount of time. Just the internal getting mixed up with the external, the emotional getting confused with the physical. That's what my mind tells me.

But my heart? It says, fuck possible.

Screw rational.

Is there anything rational about a tornado? A shooting star? A Banyan tree? No, because they're vibrant and loud, sudden and bright, messy and upside down.

Just like us.

Beautiful. Perfect. Rare and unbelievable. But not rational.

With Padraig, I don't want rational. I want the tornado.

The car winds through the roads of Rio with the ocean on our right until the driver turns into a long drive that takes us up into the hills. The villa, as my father called it, is nothing short of a mansion atop the cliff.

Padraig whistles softly as the massive stone house comes into view. "Nice place."

I barely glance at the house's façade. It's just another building to me, a showpiece in all the wrong ways. It's beautiful and expensive on the outside, but I know it will be cold and empty inside.

Just like our family.

A butler opens the door as we reach the top of the steps to a covered, stone portico. My parents are nowhere to be seen as he leads us into a side room that has been set up for a cocktail party. Tall, round tables are scattered throughout the room, and there's a bar in the far corner.

We're the only people here, but by the looks of it, we won't be for long. This isn't a dinner party. My parents are set up for a ball.

Padraig leans toward my ear. "Is this what dinner with your parents is always like?"

"Only when there's money to be made."

Heavy, purposeful footsteps echo on the marble floor of the foyer behind us, and I turn around, bracing myself. Relief floods my veins when I see who it is.

"Graham!"

My lifelong friend smiles and opens his arms. I race into them and let him pull me off my feet.

"Surprise," he laughs, setting me down.

"You said you weren't going to be able to come."

"I talked my boss into some time off."

"In other words, my father needed you down here to help sign a business deal."

Graham smiles again. "At least I'll get to see you compete."

I grab his hand and pull him into the room. "I want you to meet someone."

Padraig stands right where I left him, hands in his pockets and a cautious smile on his face. I see him through Graham's eyes for a moment—the hard angles, the dark beard, the fighter's stance. Even in his suit, Padraig couldn't look more out of place in the middle of this outlandish opulence if he tried.

"Graham, this is Padraig O'Callahan. He's a boxer from Ireland."

Padraig cocks an eyebrow at me, probably for what I'm leaving out from that introduction, but he extends his hand anyway. Graham accepts the handshake, and I'm struck with the realization that the two most important men in my life are meeting each other for the first time. It renders me momentarily speechless, so Graham finishes the introduction.

"Graham Harrison," he says. "I've known Ever since we were kids."

"Pleasure, mate," Padraig says.

"Graham's an attorney," I say. "He works for the firm that represents the hotels."

A fact that has led to some unfortunate arguments between Graham and me, but thankfully, we've figured out how to avoid most of the land mines.

"Where in Ireland are you from?" Graham asks.

"I was born in Dublin," Padraig says. "But I've spent most of my life in Galway."

I feel Graham's eyes burning a hole in my face but can't look at him.

"Galway, huh?" he says.

"Yeah, you know it?"

"I've heard about it. Ever has a strange fondness for the place."

Now I can't look at either of them.

I'm saved, if you can call it that, by the hurried click-clack of high heels on the marble. My mother breezes into the room in a swirl of Chanel No. 5 and Oscar De la Renta, her attention on the iPad in her hand.

She doesn't even look up in greeting. "Ever, thank God, you're finally here. I need your advice on where to seat that awful woman from the airline that your father said we had to invite."

I clear my throat. "Mom."

She glances up. Her practiced smile suddenly snaps into place when she sees Padraig.

"Pardon me. I didn't realize you had a friend with you."

I make the introductions again. But again I leave out the most important details—that this is the man I'm in love with.

"I'm so glad you could join us tonight, Padraig," my mother says. "The rest of our guests will arrive in the next half hour or so. Can we offer you something to drink in the meantime?"

"Not necessary, ma'am. But thank you."

"Padraig has the semi-finals tomorrow," I say. "He doesn't drink during competition."

"Really? Well, in that case, I'm so sorry Ever dragged you out here tonight with such an important competition tomorrow."

"It's no problem," he responds, his hand suddenly settling against my lower back. "It's an honor to meet Ever's family."

"Right, well, we are honored to meet you, as well," Mom says, uncharacteristically flustered. She turns to Graham. "Might I borrow you for a minute? Mitchell sent me to find you for some last-minute question before everyone arrives."

"He could come out here to see his daughter first, perhaps," Graham says tightly.

Mom looks at her feet. "Yes, well, you know how he is."

Graham snorts but follows her anyway. As soon as they leave the room, I turn to Padraig.

"I'm sorry. I didn't know how to introduce you. It sounds so stupid to say *boyfriend*, so I—"

He cuts me off with a gentle kiss, his hand on my back pressing me closer. I can feel the smile in his lips before he pulls back.

"I think they figured it out," he murmurs.

I press my forehead to his chest. "Thank you so much for being here."

"Where else would I be?"

"Resting? Getting ready for your fight? I still can't believe you agreed to be here tonight with the semi-finals tomorrow."

"Aye."

His fingers grip my chin and lift my gaze. My heart takes off in a gallop at the depth of emotion I see in his eyes.

"You didn't drag me here," he says, repeating my mother's words. "I am right where I need to be. With you."

He drops another soft kiss on my lips, lingering just long enough for me to remember what we have to look forward to when we get out of here. I want to leave now. I want him to myself.

The clock in my mind starts ticking. We only have a week left together in Rio, and I have no idea what we're going to do after that. We haven't talked about life after Rio. I haven't even told him yet about the money. And with that thought comes the panic. I should have told him before this. What if it comes up tonight? What if my father says something?

"Babe, what's wrong?" he whispers, his hand rubbing up and down my back.

"I have to tell you something."

"You can tell me anything. You know that."

I pull back and look up at him again. My mind has the words ready to go and the internal reassurances to push them out. It won't matter, my mind says. He knows me now.

But when I open my mouth, my heart goes rogue. And something else entirely comes out.

"I love you."

We both freeze. The words hang in the air, a balloon bobbing between us, waiting to pop in our faces.

I back up, my face hot, my chest tight. "I'm sorry. It's too soon. I shouldn't have said that."

Padraig grips my biceps and yanks me to him with a growl. He molds his mouth to mine and kisses me with such desire that I fist my hands against his jacket and hang on for support. His hand finds its way to the back of my head, and he tilts my face to go deeper.

He didn't say it back, but he doesn't have to. I feel it in his kiss. He loves me, too. Tears sting the back of my eyelids as I open wider to him.

"Ever!"

Oh. God.

My father.

I jump away from Padraig but keep my back turned away from my dad as I swipe a hand over my hair. Padraig doesn't let me get far. His hand grips my elbow, and he steps around me.

Shielding me.

Padraig extends his other hand toward my father. "You must be Mitchell Beckinsale."

"What the hell is going on here?" my father barks. "Ever, turn around."

I emerge from behind Padraig, face burning. Padraig lets his arm fall when it becomes clear Dad isn't going to reciprocate. He instead takes my hand in his and tugs me to his side.

It might be the most defiant display of disobedience anyone has ever attempted with my father, and I love Padraig even more for it.

"Hi, Dad," I say, meeting his eyes.

"Don't *hi* me. What the hell is this?"

My mother and Graham walk in behind him, and their eyes quickly take in the scene. My mom rushes forward.

"Mitchell, I told you Ever brought a friend," she says, coming to stand next to him.

"A *friend*?!" he barks. "That man was molesting my daughter right in the goddamned living room."

"Christ, Mitchell, "Graham groans.

Dad spins on him with a pointed finger. "You stay out of this."

I storm forward. "Who the hell do you think you are?"

"*Your father.*"

"Since when?"

"Hey, whoa." Padraig steps between us, a referee in the ring. "Let's start this over, yeah?"

He faces my dad and again extends his hand. "Padraig O'Callahan. I'm sorry we had to meet this way, but yes, I'm more than a friend."

Dad stares at Padraig's hand for a moment, and just when I think he's going to ignore the peace offering again, he returns the gesture. I let out a breath as they shake hands.

"Mitchell Beckinsale."

"Pleasure, sir." Padraig comes back to my side and tucks me in close. "But you'll have to forgive me if I can't bring myself to apologize for kissing your daughter. I'll probably even do it again some time tonight, because I find myself quite smitten with her, if that's all right with you."

I flush everywhere, and I turn my face into his arm to hide it. But not before I see my mom's mouth drop open, Graham's lips break into a grin, and my father's eyes narrow.

"Mitchell, a car is pulling into the driveway. We need to greet our guests." Mom pulls Dad away, leaving us alone with Graham.

He immediately laughs and claps Padraig on the shoulder. "This night just got interesting."

I peek up at Padraig and find him gazing down at me. The adoration in his eyes washes over me in a warm wave.

Tonight. I'm going to tell him everything tonight. And then we can plan what we're going to do after the games are over.

17

{PADRAIG}

I can't keep my hands off her.

Not when her parents drag her around the room to meet people. Not when we find ourselves cornered by "that awful woman from the airline," and not when the grim-faced butler announces that dinner is ready.

If I don't have my hand on her back or her fingers laced with mine, I make sure our bodies are touching. Never more than a breath away from each other. Because the world changed tonight.

I love you. She seemed as surprised by the words as I was, as if she intended to say something else when she first opened her mouth. Then she got a stricken look on her face and apologized, which damn near knocked me to my knees. How could she think it was the wrong thing to say?

Dinner hasn't even started yet, and I'm already dying to get out of here, take her home, and consummate the moment.

And then we'll figure out how we're going to make this work.

But first we have to get through this God-awful pretentious night. I try to focus on what people say to me during dinner, but my brain is focused entirely on Ever.

"How did you get started in boxing, Padraig?"

I blink and try to get my brain to catch up. The question is from an older American man across the table.

"I knew Billie, my coach, from around the neighborhood. He encouraged me to give it a try when I was twelve, and I've been doing it ever since."

Ever's hand glides across my leg. She obviously knows I've glossed over some of the details.

The man's wife leans forward. "Do you have any family in America?"

"Well, I don't have much family to speak of, so I don't know much about my ancestral history. But I haven't had any Americans come 'round saying they're my long lost cousin yet, so ... "

Ever's father jumps into the conversation from the head of the table.

"Ever can trace her ancestry all the way to Mayflower," he says, taking a sip from a glass of amber liquid.

"I'm duly impressed," I respond.

"That's just on her mother's side," Mitchell continues. "The Beckinsales are direct descendants of George Washington."

"You don't say." I meet his stare and refuse to look away. The man is obviously used to people cowering, but clearly he's never spent much time fighting in the alleys of Ireland.

"So besides your brother, you have no other family?" Mitchell asks.

My skin prickles with unease. "I don't recall mentioning Killian to you."

"You didn't." Mitchell takes another sip of his drink—probably some kind of pussy Protestant whiskey—and then sets down the glass. There's a deceptively satisfying gleam in his eye, like he just won a chess match I didn't know we were playing.

My fingers curl into a tight fist on my lap. The man obviously did a Google search on me. I have nothing to hide, but the fact that he dropped the information into the conversation reveals a sinister agenda.

The older woman, oblivious to the tension, smiles again. "What are your plans for after the games, Padraig?"

"An excellent question," Mitchell says.

"My plans are sort of up in the air right now."

"Up in the air," Mitchell says.

"Yes, sir."

"You haven't given any thought to life after boxing?"

"Didn't say that, sir. I have some things I'm considering."

"What kind of things?"

"The kind I'd prefer to discuss with Ever before you."

It's a wonder the man doesn't break a tooth with the way he's suddenly clenching his jaw, and the entire room suddenly settles into an uneasy silence.

Ever's hand squeezes my leg just above the knee. I look over at her and take comfort in the smile she gives me. I know I'm going to pay later with Ever's father for showing him up, but I don't care. Not as long as Ever is smiling at me.

Dinner takes forever after that. Mitchell barely acknowledges my existence, but I know it's just the calm before the storm.

As soon as the dessert dishes are cleared, people begin to rise and collect their things to leave. Ever's mom makes a beeline for us.

"Ever, I need your help. We're meeting with the tourism bureau tomorrow, and I simply cannot decide which dress to wear. Will you come look at them?"

She grabs Ever's hand and pulls her away before either of us can protest.

I'm alone.

And in Mitchell's sights.

He strolls over to me, drink in one hand and two cigars in the other. "Care to join me on the balcony for a cigar?"

"Don't smoke, sir."

"Join me anyway."

I catch Graham's eye as I follow Mitchell toward the massive French doors leading to an even more massive patio overlooking the ocean. Graham shakes his head, lips pressed into a tight line. I'm not sure if he's warning me off or apologizing in advance, but it's clear I'm walking into prize fight.

I shove my hands in my pockets and stop midway across the patio. I watch Mitchell set down his glass on a table and then deliberately light his cigar. We're like two fighters taking our corners.

Mitchell takes a deep puff and blows the smoke back in my direction. "What do you say we lay our cards on the table, Padraig?"

"I think that would be best."

He flicks nonexistent ashes. "I don't like you."

"Sorry to hear that. But all I care about is that your daughter loves me."

Mitchell cocks an eyebrow. "She loves you, does she? Did she tell you that?"

"Yes, sir."

He nods, a smirk marring his features. "She falls in love a lot."

I hold my expression and my tongue. He's trying to get a rise out of me. I won't let him.

"Can I give you some advice?" he asks.

"You can give it. Doesn't mean I'll follow it."

"Don't get your hopes up. Ever is flighty. Undisciplined. Needy. She'll suck you dry before you know it."

My hands curl into fists inside my pockets. How any man can talk about his own daughter that way is beyond me, but this is Ever. And it's a miracle I don't knock him on his ass.

"With all due respect, Mitchell, you don't seem to know your daughter at all."

"And I suppose you do?"

"I know her well enough to know that anyone who can achieve what she has at her age is the farthest thing from undisciplined and flighty a person can get. And as far as being needy, I think you're just pissed off she doesn't need you."

Mitchell pauses to take another drink from his glass. I study him like any other opponent. His pattern is clear. He tried a steady barrage of right hooks and left jabs, but I'm still standing. He'll go for the cheap shot next. It's what men like him do.

I brace myself for impact as he returns his drink to the table and faces me again with an expression of restrained fury.

"Let me be absolutely clear, Padraig," he says.

"Please do."

"I don't care how my daughter feels about you, but I can tell you with absolute certainty that no uneducated street fighter with a brother in prison for murder is going to see a dime of her trust fund. I will cut her out of the will entirely before I let that happen."

That wasn't a cheap shot. That was a full-on sucker punch, because I have no fucking idea what he's talking about. What trust fund?

My expression brings a victorious gleam to his eyes. "You don't know what I'm talking about, do you?"

Sweat pools under my arms, and Billie's voice echoes in my ears. *How much do you know about this girl?*

"Come now, Padraig," Mitchell says, smiling. "Don't play dumb with me. Surely someone who is such an important part of my daughter's life is aware of her financial situation."

I finally cave. "What the hell are you on about?"

Mitchell's laugh is like ice. "Ever's grandparents left her a trust fund. It will settle on her birthday next month, all three hundred and fifty million dollars of it."

The words are an uppercut. A brain-shaking blow to the chin. There has to be a mistake. I must have heard him wrong, misunderstood the words.

Mitchell laughs again. "I warned you, son. You can't trust her. If she didn't even tell you this, it makes you wonder how much she actually loves you, doesn't it?"

It's a knock-out blow, like he knew just where to hit to finish me off.

She didn't tell me. Ever knew this entire time she was about to inherit more money than I can even fathom, and she never mentioned it once.

How much do you know about this girl?

Maybe nothing at all.

18

{EVER}

He knows.

I can tell as soon as they walk back in. Padraig's body language broadcasts the truth through the grim line of his lips, the tense square of his shoulders, and the stiff gait of his walk.

But even if I couldn't tell from Padraig, I would know the instant I looked at my father. He smiles like a prosecutor who just nailed a suspect on the stand. The triumphant set of his eyes makes my stomach pitch.

He actually enjoys this. Ruining my life is a game to him. I'm nothing more than a business competitor to defeat any way he can.

When I look at Padraig again, I know my father has won.

The man who just two hours ago hauled me against him and kissed me like I was the air he breathes now stands apart from me —a few feet, but it might as well be a thousand. The eyes that once never strayed from mine now dart around the room, looking everywhere but at me. The hands that have sought me out all night now hang by his sides in tight balls of anger.

He looks exactly like the man I found on the balcony the first night in Rio.

"What did he tell you?" I manage to say.

A vein pops in his jaw. "Enough."

The air rushes from my lungs. Sweat pools under my arms as my heart cracks in my chest. The walls close in on me, and I react the only way I know how.

I spin on my heel and leave.

I race out the front door but barely make it across the porch before I hear his footsteps following me.

"Ever!"

There's no tenderness in his voice.

I jog down the cement steps as fast as my heels allow. I search for the driver of our car, but he has already spotted us and is jogging our way.

"I'm ready to go," I say.

He nods and jogs back toward the car.

Padraig catches up with me. He grips my elbow and spins me around. "How could you keep something like that from me?"

"I was going to tell you tonight." It sounds lame even to my own ears, even if it's the truth.

"You should have told me from the start, Ever."

"Why?"

He makes a noise, a cross between incredulous grunt and an are-you-fucking-kidding-me laugh. The car pulls up in front of us, and I don't bother to wait for the driver to get out and open my door.

I yank on the handle, but Padraig's arm shoots out and holds it shut.

"Are you seriously *leaving*?"

"You left me the minute you walked back in with my father."

He doesn't deny it, and I break into a thousand pieces inside. Oh my God. This can't be happening. I told him I loved him, and it wasn't enough. I'm never enough.

I open the door and slide into the backseat.

His face hardens and he climbs in after me, slamming the door shut behind him. The car starts to move.

I stare out the window as the driver turns onto the road at the bottom of the hill.

"Ever, you can't expect me to not be mad. You *lied* to me."

"No, I didn't. I just hadn't told you everything yet."

"Same thing."

"I didn't mean for you to find out this way. I'm sorry. I really was going to tell you." The tone of my voice makes me wince. I'm clingy. Needy. Emotional.

"You should have seen your father's face. I've never seen anyone gloat as much as he did when he realized I had no fucking idea what he was talking about."

"I'm sorry." The apology is automatic, but I know it won't matter.

"I just don't understand why you kept this a secret. After everything we've talked about, how could you not mention something this important?"

I somehow find the strength to tear my gaze from the window. "Why does it matter so much?"

"It's three hundred and fifty million dollars! How is that not important?"

"It's just money, Padraig."

"Just money? The only people who throw around the words *it's just money* are people who've never had to live without it."

His sarcasm stings like salt to a wound. "Perhaps you've forgotten how I've been living for two years."

He snorts. "Right. You're destitute."

"You knew I was going to inherit money someday when my parents die. What difference does it make if I get three hundred and fifty million now instead of a billion dollars later?"

He blinks rapidly and then barks out a joyless laugh. "You have to be kidding me. Do you even know how you sound right now?"

I look at my lap. "Like a spoiled rich girl?"

"Yes!"

I wince at the anger behind that one word. The car slows in front of the athlete's condo. I throw open the door and jump out. Padraig calls my name, and I hear his own door open and slam shut behind me as I race across the concrete sidewalk toward the building.

It takes him mere seconds to catch up with me. "No way, Ever. You're not running out on this conversation. Not again."

I gape at him as I pull open the heavy glass door. "*Again?*"

"This is what you do. You run away when things get hard. It's what you did that very first night. It's what you did fifteen minutes ago."

His words slice through me, and I stammer as I push the button for the elevator.

"I ran away from you that first night because I knew there was no point in trying to explain," I say. "Just like tonight. You've already made up your mind."

"How can I make up my mind when I have no idea if you're being honest with me?"

For the second time tonight, my lungs deflate. I blink at him, shattering inside. "I was honest about everything that matters," I whisper. "I was honest when I said I love you."

The elevator opens and is blissfully empty when we walk in. As soon as the door slides shut, I hug one wall and he clings to the other. The space between us yawns like the Grand Canyon—big, wide, impossible to cross. I suddenly wish for a crowd to hide in.

Padraig lets out a long breath and looks at his feet for a moment. Then he scrubs his hand over his hair.

"It's late," he says, finding something fascinating in his shoes. "I need proper rest for the semi-finals. Maybe it would best if I slept back in my own apartment tonight."

"OK." *Not OK. Oh my God, not OK.*

He must have heard something in my voice, because he looks up. "I just think maybe we need to cool down while we think about things."

"You need to think about things?" Needy. Clingy. Melodramatic.

"Don't you?"

The elevator stops. I dart into the hallway, not bothering to wait for him. The sounds of loud sex from a nearby apartment make my cheeks flush with heat and embarrassment. Could people hear us from my room when we made love?

Wait. *My* room.

Oh God. It's really happening. It doesn't even feel like *our* room anymore.

My hands shake as I search for my keys in my purse.

"I've got it," he says quietly, reaching around me from behind. He shoves his key in the lock and gives it a twist. The door swings open. I practically run inside, desperate for space.

He follows more slowly, a weary sigh filling the silence. I cross the room to the kitchen and busy myself fetching a bottle of water from the fridge. I'm not thirsty, but I need the distraction.

I twist the top off and slosh water on myself as my trembling hands raise the bottle to my lips.

"I'll wait out here while you get your things," I say, setting the bottle down, picking at the label.

He doesn't respond, so I look up. His brows are pulled tightly together, his lips parted.

"I don't need my stuff, Ever," he says. "It's just one night."

"Maybe it should be more."

He hardens. "Is that what you want?"

"It's what you want."

"I never said that."

"But that's what you need to think about, isn't it?"

He grips the back of his neck and then lets his arm fall with an angry jerk. "Is this what you're going to do every time we have a fight? Shut down and throw me out?"

"You're the one who said it would be better if you slept in your own apartment."

"Jesus! You're acting like a—" He stops himself.

"Say it," I snap.

"A spoiled rich girl."

"That's all I am to you now, right?" I round the counter separating the kitchen from the living room. "That's what's really bothering you. It's not that I kept it from you. It's not even the money itself. It's how the money makes you see me. You only want the Ever who cries by the water. You only want the Ever who lives in a loft above a horse barn. You don't want Ever the rich girl."

"I never said that," he repeats, this time through a clenched jaw.

"You didn't have to. I have eyes, Padraig. You're looking at me the same way you looked at me that first night. That's why I didn't tell you. Because I couldn't stand for you to look at me that way again."

My mind pleas with him to tell me I'm wrong. He just blinks, expression unreadable.

"Just tell me *why*," I beg, not even bothering to hide the needy tone of my voice. "Why do you hate the rich girl part of me so much?"

"Because they cost me everything!"

The words explode from his mouth and send shrapnel of truth and understand everywhere. He does have a reason. I knew it. And it matters.

"Who did? What did they do?"

"Killian is in prison because of a rich bastard who lied and pinned everything on him. He walked away while my brother rots in a prison cell."

"And you think it's because he's rich that he got away with it?"

"I know it's because he's rich! There are no fuckin' laws for the rich."

The shrapnel wounds start to bleed. "And you wonder why I didn't want you to know about the money."

He whips around and stomps to the bedroom. Drawers bang. The closet door slams. I close my eyes when I hear him cross the hallway to the bathroom.

Finally, he emerges, his stuffed duffel bag over his shoulder. He drops it to the floor and paves a quick path toward me. I back up until my butt collides with the counter.

I barely have time to react before he cups my face and crushes his mouth to mine. His kiss is hard and punishing. When he finally wrenches his mouth from mine, he's panting as fast as I am.

"Ever, I love you, but I …"

I freeze. My entire body soars at *I love you*, but then crashes at the next word.

But.

The one word I fear most. The one word that has defined my life.

Darling, we'd love to see you jump, but...

Of course we miss you when you're at school, but...

I want to marry you, but...

I love you, but ...

I thought I couldn't feel any worse than I already did, but I was wrong. I'm bleeding out.

I slide away from him and turn my face. "Don't say that."

"I can't even tell you I love you?"

"You said 'I love you, *but...*' There's no in-between, Padraig. You either love all of me or you don't."

"That's not fair."

"You should go."

"No. Look at me."

"*Go.*"

I turn around and grip the edge of the counter. I can't watch him leave. I want to squeeze my eyes shut and have someone tell me when it's over.

He stalks to the living room, and I hear him lift the bag. Pieces of me crumble and fall with every step that takes him to the front door.

He pauses there. "Just so I'm clear, I need to know what's happening here."

I barely glance over my shoulder. "Good luck tomorrow."

He hovers a moment, and just when I'm tempted to turn around and run to him, he walks out.

The click of the door behind him echoes with a finality that sends me to the floor.

I've felt alone all my life.

But *lonely* has never hurt like this.

19

{PADRAIG}

YOU DON'T FIGHT MAD.

Rage is the easy way out. It's cheap and dirty. It's for back-alley brawlers who end up behind bars, not with medals around their necks.

It took years of Billie grabbing me by the shirt and screaming it in my face before I eventually learned the difference between fighting with my fists and fighting with my head.

But today, I fought mad.

I fought with rage in my fists.

I fought cheap and dirty, because that's who I am. I left the only good part of me in an apartment on the sixth floor, and this is what's left.

Now, I'm sitting on the bench in front of my locker in the arena, hands still taped, sweat dripping from my brow to the floor, my veins still pulsing with fury.

In a room down the hallway, the press waits for me.

On the seat next to me, so does Billie.

"What happened," he finally says.

"I won."

"That wasn't a victory. That was a beating."

"I got the job done, didn't it?"

"You're not here to get a job done. You're here to represent your country, your club, and yourself. And that display out there was nothing to be proud of."

I shoot to my feet. "I'm fighting for the gold tomorrow. What else do you want from me?"

"To stop fighting the man in the mirror."

"Jesus," I groan, ripping at the tape on my hands. "Not this shite again."

"Something happened with your girl, didn't it?"

My chest tightens. "Feel free to say *I told you so*. I know you want to."

"I don't. I want to know if you're OK."

"I'm fine."

"Padraig, look at me."

I take my time turning around. Billie reaches his hands toward mine, and I let him take over on the tape.

"Why do you think I made you promise me you'd keep your shite in line this time?" he asks.

"Because it's your last chance to say you trained a gold medalist."

He tosses the tape. "Fer fuck's sake, Paddy. Do ya' really think I care that much about a fuckin' gold medal for myself?"

I snap my gaze to his.

"I worry about *you*, Paddy. I need ya' to win the gold for *you*. The only person you let down in London was yourself. Maybe you don't remember what a mess ya' were after those games, but I do."

He's wrong. I do remember. But then I met a woman by the bay who changed everything. A woman I've lost again.

Billie points toward the door. "The man I saw in the ring today was the same man who came home from London. Broken. Angry. We might be one fight away from a gold medal, son, but I'm afraid there aren't enough medals in the world for you to put your past behind you and respect yourself."

I face my locker, because it's easier than facing him.

"Look," he says. "I wasn't going to tell you this yet. Not until after Rio. But I think maybe you need to hear it now."

"Tell me what?"

"I want you to take over the club."

My brain is slow to process his words, my body even slower to turn around. "What do you mean?"

"I'm giving it to ya'. The gym. I want you keep it alive after I retire, take over as a coach. I know you'll be a good one."

"You want *me*?"

"I met with my solicitors a few months ago. Got the paperwork all drawn up. All you have to do is sign, and it's yours."

I sink against my locker. "I don't know what to say, Billie."

"You don't have to say anything right now. I just wanted ya' to know."

I manage to nod or something like it.

Billie wheezes as he struggles to stand. "I don't know what happened with you and the Beckinsale girl, but I do know you're better than what you did out there today. And while you're prob-ably standing there telling yourself you performed like that because of her, it's a lie. You're sabotaging yourself just like ya' did in London, because deep down, you don't believe you deserve any of this. And that's not something I can coach out of ya'. That's something only you can fix."

He hacks a couple of times and then lightly pounds his fist on my shoulder. I hang my head as I listen to him shuffle out. My muscles are Jell-O. My chest a gaping hole.

I turn around and bracket my locker with my hands. Billie wants me to take over the gym. It's the greatest statement of faith anyone has ever made about me. I didn't go to university. I barely graduated from secondary. But he trusts me to carry on his legacy. Even when I act like a fuck-up.

You're better than what you did out there today.

The words ring hollow, because I don't know if I actually believe them.

I sink back down on the bench, weariness sucking the last strains of strength from my legs. I plant my elbows on my knees and press my forehead into my hands. Is Billie right? Am I sabotaging myself?

I fucked things up so badly last night. The way Ever looked at me—the betrayal in her eyes—has haunted me every second since I walked out on her.

Jesus. Billie *is* right. I am sabotaging myself, because I don't believe I deserve this. Any of this. The Olympics. The gold medal. The fame. *Ever.*

The fact is, every time I step in the ring, every time I throw a punch, I'm fighting against myself, who I used to be and fear I still am—a man who doesn't deserve a woman like her.

My breaths start coming fast and hard like I just went another nine rounds. What the fuck have I done? I let Ever push me away last night because it was easier than facing the truth. The money didn't change how I see her. I panicked because I was terrified that it will change how *she* sees *me*.

No wonder she didn't tell me about the money. Ever knew me better than I knew myself. I *did* prefer the Ever who lives in a loft above a horse barn, because I can live there, too. But I have no fucking idea how to live in her gilded world. I don't belong there, and I let her father poke me right where it hurts. I let him give credence to the doubts and the fear that she'd figure out sooner or later that I'm not good enough for her.

I let the fear take over and threaten the best thing that ever happened to me.

The door to the locker room swings open, and one of the team's publicists sticks his head in. "Aye, mate. The press is waitin'."

I wave him off.

Ten minutes. That's all I'll give them, because I have something far more important to do.

I have to win back my girl.

Because even if I win the gold tomorrow, I will have won nothing if I've lost her.

I shower and change into my official Irish track suit, mentally practicing the canned, bullshite answers I'll give to the media so I can get out of there as fast as possible.

But as soon as I hoist my duffel bag over my shoulder, the door to the locker room slams open again. Billie barrels inside, his eyes dark.

"Fer fuck's sake, I'm comin'," I snap.

Billie holds up his hands. "Ever was in an accident."

20

{PADRAIG}

A ROARING SOUND in my ears blocks out everything Billie says after *accident*. I see his mouth moving, but I hear nothing. Then he hands me his phone, his browser called up to a grainy video.

I press the triangle in the middle. My stomach sours and squeezes as I watch shaky footage of the woman I love rounding the training course and preparing for a jump.

Suddenly, Bobby McGee's back feet clip the line. He stumbles on the landing. Ever flies over the top of him. Lands on her right shoulder.

And doesn't move.

I cover my mouth with my hand, even as my eyes focus on the timestamp. A growl erupts from my throat.

"This was four hours ago!"

Billie shakes his head. "We were in black-out, Padraig."

I drop my bag and dig my phone out. Fuck. FUCK. "Who turned my fucking phone off?"

"I did." He swallows, apologetic.

I grab my bag, plow past him into the hallway, and hold the button to power up my phone.

"I'm sorry, Paddy," Billie says, shuffling to keep up behind me. "I didn't want you to be distracted before the fight."

The hallway is crowded with Olympics staffers and athletes, all of whom want to stop me and congratulate me. I push past them all, staring at my phone and willing it back to life.

Finally, the screen lights up and immediately starts to blow up with notifications.

Six missed calls, all from a U.S. number I don't recognize.

Then a string of texts from the same number.

I dodge another group of staffers calling my name as I swipe the first text, sent three hours before my fight.

Padraig-It's Graham. Call me asap.

I don't bother to read the rest of the texts. I hit the call back button, press the phone to my ear, and slam my hand against the heavy metal doors to the outside.

Graham answers almost immediately.

I skip the greetings and step into the sun. "How is she?"

"She broke her arm in two places and has a mild concussion."

The air rushes from my lungs, and I have to bend and grip my knee to keep from stumbling. A confusing blend of relief and horror sends my stomach into my throat.

"Broken arm," I pant. "She can't…"

"No," Graham says, voice clipped. "She can't compete."

I stand and feel Billie take my bag from me. "Where is she now?"

"They just released her. She's going to the equestrian center to wait for word on Bobby McGee."

I stumble again. "What about him?"

"They're concerned about his leg."

Leg injuries in horses can be a death sentence. My stomach threatens again. "She can't lose that horse, Graham."

"I know," he says softly before going silent for a moment. Then, "I'll make sure you can get in."

"Thank you."

We end the call, and I turn to Billie. I fill him in on Ever's injuries as he flags down a security guard in an SUV. He must've read my mind. I don't have time to wait for a shuttle. The equestrian center is a half hour by car at this time of day. By shuttle, it would take us an hour.

I explain everything to the security guard the best I can, and even though he doesn't speak English, he's clearly fluent in urgent facial expressions. He just nods and motions for me to get in. I take my bag from Billie and climb into the front seat.

I immediately dial Ever's phone number and stare out the window, knee shaking, while I wait for her to answer.

It goes straight to voicemail, so I switch to texting.

Babe…I'm on my way.

I stare at my phone, willing her to respond.

She doesn't.

I had my phone off. I'm so sorry.

Minutes pass. No response.

I clench my phone and contemplate throwing it out the window.

Self-recriminations pummel me left and right like I've been backed into the corner.

I should have called this morning.

I should have told my pride to shut it.

I should have fucking stayed!

The slow, stop-and-go ride is agony, and I torture myself by watching the video over and over again. My body stiffens every time I watch her fall. I feel the jolt in my bones, the fear in my gut.

Finally, the equestrian center comes into view. The guard barely slows before I throw open the door with a thank you. Adrenaline fills my limbs with a surge of strength as I race toward the entrance that Ever took me in the first time.

Security guards hold up their hands and tell me to stop.

"Padraig O'Callahan," I pant. "I'm with Ever Beckinsale."

They consult an iPad while I grit my teeth. Then one of them nods and waves me through. I take off running again, dodging horses, people, and piles of shit as I race toward the main corridor.

I hear my name and skid to a stop, looking around. Graham jogs toward me.

"She's meeting with the veterinarians," he says.

"Any word yet?"

Graham shakes his head, his lips pressed into a tight line.

"If there's a break, will they have to put him down?" I can't even stand to say the words.

"They don't know yet."

"They can't, Graham. She'll never survive it."

"I know."

He stares at me silently again, studying me, and I let him. I deserve the scrutiny.

"You really love her, don't you?" he finally says.

"Yes."

"I'm in love with her, too, you know."

I figured that already, but hearing him say it is like having him reach into my chest and yank out my heart. He's everything I'm not. He was born into her world.

He steps closer and lowers his voice. "But the problem with Ever is that she doesn't know how to be loved. She doesn't trust it. All her life she's been taught that she will always come second with the people who are supposed to care. Her parents. Her fiancé. They taught her that other things will always matter more."

Something clicks in my mind. *You said I love you, but...*

Oh, fuck. It's worse than I feared. Everything about last night was a test, one I failed in epic fashion. I lost her the instant I made her believe there were conditions to my feelings. Instead of holding her when she lashed out, what did I do? I told her she wasn't being fair, and I left.

My chest, already aching, caves in on itself.

"I don't know what happened between you two last night after you left, but I know Ever, and I know that she has a habit of pushing people away before they can do the same to her." Graham pauses and runs his hands over his jaw. "Just promise me you won't let her get away with it. If you're strong enough to do that, I won't stand in your way, and I'll make damn sure her parents don't, either."

My tongue is thick in my mouth. "Why are you helping me?"

"Because I want her to be happy." He swallows hard. "And because I'm smart enough to know she'll never love me the same way she loves you."

Hope flutters in my stomach. "She told you she loves me?"

His mouth tips up into a sad smile. "She didn't have to."

He steps back and points down the corridor. "They should be out soon."

I bounce my bag further on my shoulder, and start to run again. The corridor is teeming with life as I jog toward Bobby's stall.

Stable hands scurry up and down the long hallway carrying buckets, halters, and other tools of the trade. The clip-clop of hooves echo against the walls as Olympians lead horses to their stalls. Groomers tend to manes and tails, while staffers replace dirty hay with fresh.

My eyes take it all in as yet another painful realization hits me. *This* is Ever's world. *This* is where she calls home, trust fund or no trust fund. My own insecurities blinded me to so much, and if that stupidity has cost me the woman I love, I will never get over it.

I stop short when I see her standing at Bobby McGee's stall. Just like the first time I saw her, the air seeps from my lungs. Her muscular legs are encased in white riding pants and tall black boots. Her hair is pulled back in some kind of elaborate braid, exposing all the places on her long neck my lips ache to taste again. Her right arm is tucked closed to her body in a sling, and I have to bite back a full-fledged whimper at the sight of it.

She's so focused on murmuring to Bobby McGee, her lips pressed to his nose, that she doesn't even notice me until I'm standing just a few feet away. She glances in my direction and then quickly does a double take.

"Padraig," she breathes. "How—how'd you get in here?"

So much for a kiss-filled reunion. I drop my bag. "Graham let me in."

I step closer but stop when her shoulders tense. She's a skittish foal again, scared of me. My body aches to hold her, but her body screams BACK OFF.

This is what I've done. She's a foot away, but it might as well be a million miles. She's not the Ever who clung to me in the shower or the Ever who blurted *I love you.* She's the Ever who faced me with a weary scowl when I tried to apologize the first time so many days ago.

I want *my* Ever back.

"Babe," I somehow manage to say over the growing lump in my throat. "I'm so sorry."

She turns back to the horse, but not before I see her bottom lip tremble.

"For what?" she asks too casually.

"Everything. Are you OK?"

"I'm fine."

"What about Bobby?"

She rubs his nose. "He's OK. It's not a break."

My chest empties with a relieved breath. "Thank God."

She nods and forces a fake smile. "Congratulations on the win today."

"Christ, Ever. I don't care about boxing right now."

I move closer until my body brushes hers. Her lips quiver again but then tighten. A pair of stable hands walk by, watching us closely. I wait until they pass before doing what I've been dying to do since I saw her standing here. I touch her. I wrap my fingers about the back of her neck and rub my thumb against her silky skin.

"Babe, please look at me."

The muscles of her throat work against a hard swallow but she refuses to meet my gaze.

"I shouldn't have left last night," I say, my voice barely recognizable. "You were right about me. I was scared shitless about how the money would change things between us, and I was a fucking idiot for that. But the one thing it never changed is how much I love you."

"You love me, *but*," she whispers.

"No." I press my forehead to her temple. "I love you *period*."

Her body shakes against mine, and her chest convulses with a suppressed sob. I slip my arm around her waist, careful to avoid her arm, and then press my lips to her neck, to her ear, to her hair. I close my eyes and inhale the essence of her—the mingling, maddening scents of saddle and sun, lavender and life.

"I'm so sorry, Ever. I'm never going to let you go again. I don't care about the money. I don't care if—"

"I'm leaving tomorrow."

The words hit me like a left jab to the ribcage and have the same effect. I stumble, breathless, and my hand falls to my side. "What—what do you mean?"

"I'm going home."

"B-but the games aren't over."

"They're over for me."

Her voice breaks, and so does my fucking soul.

"My parents are done with their business stuff, and I'm going to fly back with them."

I've only been knocked out in the ring once. It felt a lot like this. One minute you're on your feet and holding your own, and in the next you're confused and spinning inside your own brain. I plant my hands on the top of my head. This can't be happening. She can't leave.

I reach for her again. "Babe, don't do this."

She dodges my touch. "It's for the best, Padraig. You know it is."

"Best for who?"

"Both of us."

"Bullshit."

She jerks her gaze to mine. "What?"

"You're running away again."

Her lips tighten. "You ran away from me last night."

It's another test, one I refuse to fail again. "You're right. I did. I let you push me away because I was a coward. But I'm not going to let you do it again."

I watch in horror as her eyes crest, as twin tears slip their barriers and slide down her cheeks. "It's too late."

"No," I choke out. "We waited two years for each other. It's not too late."

Her hands wipe at the tears. "I came here to win a gold medal, and I failed. You and I had something really beautiful and special for a very short amount of time, but now it's over."

She turns her back on me, walks to Bobby McGee, and presses her face to his, seeking comfort from the one and only thing she fully trusts.

I've known every kind of pain there is. The physical pain of fist pounding flesh. The emotional pain of guilt and hopelessness. Even the gut-wrenching, hollowed-out pain of loss.

But this pain—the pain of two simple words, *it's over*—might kill me.

"Is that all that matters to you? The gold medal?"

She stills but doesn't turn around.

It takes all my strength to hold my voice steady as I talk to her stiff back. "I thought the only thing that mattered to me was winning the gold, too, but that was before you tackled me in the bathroom. And now none of this matters without you."

I take a chance. I reach out and touch her back. "I know you're afraid, and I know it's because I've let you down. I'm sorry I didn't realize sooner that the absolute worst thing I could've done last night was walk away from you. I should have fought harder."

I have to stop and breathe.

"But I also know that I love you. I've loved you for two years, and I will love you forever. And when you're ready to forgive me and trust me and meet me half way, I'll be waiting."

I look at my feet, eyes blurry. The last part ... I know I need to say it, but Jesus, I'm scared.

"The thing is, Ever, I need you to fight for me, too."

I reach into my pocket and pull out the Claddagh stone. It doesn't belong to me anymore. I set it on the small stool next to the gate. Then I pick up my bag and turn away. My hands curl into fists at the sound of her quietly crying behind me, but I don't stop. Walking away from her last night was an act of cowardice. Tonight, it's one of necessity.

I can't force her. I can't beg her. I can only wait for her.

And I will.

For Ever, I can wait forever.

21

{EVER}

I HOLD it in for hours.

I keep the pain and the tears shoved down inside me while I prepare Bobby McGee to travel, while I pack up my room one-armed, while I crawl into bed and thank God for the painkillers to help me sleep.

I hold it in as I cross the lobby to the shuttle that will take me to the airport the next morning, while my eyes search for him with every step.

I hold it in until the private Beckinsale jet takes off from the runway with a whine and a stomach-tugging pull away from gravity.

Only then do I look at the window, clutch the Claddagh stone, and let out it all out. I press my face to the cool pane and try to sob quietly. I'm in the farthest seat in the back, alone. My parents will

soon pass-out from a couple of gin-and-tonics and the lull of the
air. Graham has barely spoken to me, except for the politest courte-
sies. I muffle my crying anyway, because I don't want to risk any
of them hearing me.

If they heard me, they would ask what's wrong, and I'm not
sure I can explain it. I hurt everywhere. I'm just not sure why. I'm
making the right decision. I have to leave. So why does it hurt
so bad?

"Ever."

I jump at the warmth of Graham's hand on my shoulder. Shit. I
keep my face turned away and wipe madly at my wet cheeks with
my good hand.

"Hey," he says quietly, sitting down in the empty seat beside.
He wraps his arm around me and tugs me gently to his chest. "It's
OK. You can cry."

He seems as surprised as I am when I bury my face against him
and sob. Before Rio, I would have pretended I was fine. But I'm
not the same person I was then. I'll never be her again.

Graham wraps his other arm around my back and holds me.
But after a moment, he surprises me, too.

"Ever, what the fuck are you doing?"

I pull back and hiccup. "What?"

His eyes are warm but disappointed. "What are you doing on
this plane?"

I wipe my face again. "Going home."

"Yeah, but why?"

"Because it's over."

"What's over?"

"The games! I came here to win a gold medal, and I failed."
Why is that so hard for everyone to understand?

A rare flash of anger crosses his face. "Who gives a shit about the games?"

When he speaks again, it's as if the words are actually painful.

"There is a man down there who loves you. He loves you even more than I do, and I didn't think that was possible."

My mouth drops open and a squeak falls out.

"For years, I've watched you go from one shithead to the next. I even had to watch you get engaged to one, and if you don't think that was torture, you don't know what torture is. But every time, I knew it would fall apart and you'd let me pick up the pieces. And I didn't mind. Because yes, I love you."

My chest cracks. "Graham ... I didn't know."

He waves his hands. "It doesn't matter. That's not the point." He lets out a frustrated breath. "The point is, I honestly never believed you'd find someone who actually deserved you, but you did. But now I'm not sure you deserve him."

I sink back against my seat, his words stealing my breath and my voice.

He sighs, dragging his fingers through his hair. "I know your story better than pretty much anyone. I know what it's been like for you with those two—" He gestures toward the front of the plane. "—as your parents. But aren't you tired of letting them control your life?"

"Excuse me?" Defensiveness makes me sit straighter. "I have spent two years living in a shithole above a horse barn because I refuse to let them control my life! I've devoted everything to a sport I love in *defiance* of them. How dare you—"

He covers my mouth with his hand. "Why do you want a gold medal?"

I smack his hand away with my one good one. "You know why."

"To prove them wrong?"

"Yes!"

"And so you can live your life the way you want."

I nod. It sounds stupid and shallow when he says it, but it's true, and I can't deny it.

"Dammit, Ever!"

His uncharacteristic outburst makes me jump in my seat.

"How long are you going to lie to yourself? You didn't want a gold medal so you could *leave* your family and live your life the way you want to. Just the opposite. You hoped it would make them beg you to stay, to say they are proud of you. You hoped it would make them love you."

He might as well have slapped me. I shake my head in tiny, frantic movements. "Shut up."

"Why? Afraid of the truth."

"It's not the truth!"

"Why do you need a gold medal to live your life on your own terms? You're an adult, Ever, and as of next month, you'll have more money than you could spend in a lifetime. Take it and flip them the finger, if that's that what you want. But you can't, can you? Because you're afraid that if you do, they'll never want you back."

The crack in my chest becomes a chasm. "How can you say this to me?"

"Because I'm your friend. And I want you to stop fighting things you can't change. You'll never change them, Ever. They love you in their own way, the only way they know how, but we both know it's not enough. You're going to walk away from someone who would die for you to chase after two people who have made it clear you're an afterthought in their lives and always have been."

Tears threaten again as I look at my lap, ashamed of the disappointment I see reflected in Graham's gaze, crushed by the harsh truth of his words. It's not that I didn't know that about my parents. But knowing someone else sees it, too, is like being stripped naked in front of a crowd.

Graham reaches over and takes my hand.

"I don't like saying these things to you, honey. I hate seeing you hurt. But you're going to be hurt a thousand times more if you walk away from Padraig."

"He hurt me, Graham," I choke. "He freaked out about the money—"

"So what? He made a mistake. He'll probably make a thousand more, but so will you."

"It's not about mistakes. The money is always going to be between us."

"Only if you let it. And only if you're too scared to forgive him."

I close my eyes as Padraig's voice fills my ears.

I've loved you for two years, and I will love you forever. And when you're ready to forgive me and trust me and meet me halfway, I'll be waiting ... The thing is, Ever, I need you to fight for me, too.

My eyes fly open.

Oh my God. Graham is right.

I've been blaming him for leaving, but I pushed him out. I've been blaming him for being mad about the money, but I didn't give him a chance to explain his fears.

I've been blaming him for the fight, but the fight is what might have saved us if I'd only fought back.

I treated him like my parents have always treated me.

"What have I done," I whisper.

"Nothing that can't be undone."

I lean forward and kiss Graham's cheek. Then I leap to my feet and run to the front. The private flight attendant looks up with a gentle smile.

"Can I help you, Miss Beckinsa—"

"Turn the plane around."

22

{EVER}

RUNNING toward something feels better than running away.

And running is what I'm doing. Literally. Running toward the boxing pavilion, every step jarring my broken arm but healing my broken heart.

Graham huffs and puffs next to me, phone pressed to his ear, barking out orders like my father trained him to.

"Have them meet us at the south entrance," he snaps. "We're not leaving until someone lets us in."

Even if Lorna and Quinn come through and manage to get us in without tickets, there will still be only a few minutes for me to see Padraig before the fight begins.

Pride overtakes panic when I picture him on the podium, the Irish national anthem playing while they loop a medal around his neck.

I can't miss it.

I can't lose him.

I can't believe I left.

My father threw a fit about turning around, and frankly, I'm not sure when I'll speak to him again, but Mom—wonder of wonders —stood up for me. I'll thank her later. The only thing I can think about right now is getting to Padraig.

Sweat trickles down my back as we round the corner of the building. I nearly collapse in relief as I watch the door swing open and Lorna walk out. She spots us immediately and waves.

"We only have five minutes!" she shouts.

Hopefully, that's all I need. Graham and I follow her inside, and the three of us run down a long, cinderblock hallway.

"Does he know I'm here?" I pant.

Lorna shakes her head. "Billie said I couldn't tell him."

"But Billie will let me see him, right?"

Lorna skids to a stop in front of a locker room door. "He's the one who told me to let you in."

I grip the handle of the door with my good hand and yank it open.

It's silent inside. My footsteps echo eerily on the tile floor as I cross the entry into the main locker room.

He sits alone on a bench, his back to me, elbows resting on his knees and his head pressed into his hands. Athletes have all kinds of pre-competition rituals, and this is his. Sitting alone. Picturing the fight. Centering himself.

I don't want to interrupt, but I have to.

"Padraig?"

Just like the night on the balcony, his shoulders tense at the sound of my voice.

But unlike the night on the balcony, I'm not going to hesitate.

"Can I join you?" I say.

He moves in slow motion. His head swivels to look over his shoulder. His mouth drops open. His eyes grow wide and round.

"Ever?" He says my name like he's afraid he's hallucinating.

"I'm here."

He stands and turns toward me. "I thought you left."

"I did. I came back."

"Why?"

"Because I love you," I cross the room until I'm inches away from him and staring up in those eyes that make me tremble. "And because you were right about me. I'm a coward who has run away from everything my whole life, but now I'm running to you, and I hope I'm not too late. I hope I haven't ruined this—"

He cups my face with this boxing gloves and kisses me. Deep. Hard. Hungry. He kisses me like a man drowning, and I'm his first gulp of air. He kisses me until my knees get weak with joy, and the only thing holding me up is the strength of his love.

I wrap my good arm around his neck and lean into him and open myself wider, apologizing with my whole body. It's just us. Nothing else matters. Gold or no gold. We'll figure it out and make it work.

"Wait." He pulls back.

My stomach drops. "Wh-what's wrong?"

He laughs and shakes his head. "We need to figure this out, but I don't have time right now. I just need you to know that Billie offered to turn the club over to me, but that means living in Galway, and I know your horses are in Kentucky."

This time I cut *him* off with a kiss. I breathe forgiveness into every press of my lips against his. "We'll figure it out," I whisper. "*Together.*"

"God, Ever," he groans, pressing his forehead to mine. "I really thought I'd lost you."

I laugh through tears and shake my head.

"It's OK now," I whisper against his lips. "Because I found you."

EPILOGUE

One year later

{PADRAIG}

MY PHONE SCREECHES on the table next to the bed, and I damn near break my arm scrambling to grab it.

"It's time." Ever's voice is breathless. "Drive as fast as you can."

"Shite, honey. Just hang on. I'm on my way."

I can't miss this. I can't miss the birth of our first baby. Ever will never forgive me, and I'll never forgive myself. I shove my feet into some shoes and throw on a t-shirt and am racing out the front door before I realize I forgot my keys.

I spin back around on the front porch of our nearly finished home outside Galway and burst back through the door. Keys. Keys. Where are my feckin' keys?!

Oh. Right where I left them last night when I got home because Ever insisted I wasn't needed yet. I knew I should've stayed, but she kissed me and looked at me in that way that can get me to do anything, and now here I am ... leaping off the porch and nearly face-planting on the freshly paved driveway.

"Rio!" I yell. Our six-month-old Border Collie follows me out of the house at full puppy speed.

The sun barely peeks over the horizon as I race up the road in our new truck with Beckinsale Stables painted on the side. A pink glow bathes the countryside in the calm of the coming dawn, but my heart races like a galloping stallion. I'm only ten minutes away, but I feel every second like I'm getting my arse kicked in the ring.

Finally, the road comes into view. The truck barely stays on all four wheels as I peel around the corner. It's a long drive, nearly a mile back. In the pasture to my right, Bobby McGee runs alongside my truck, his mane wild and free. Rio barks at the sight of his best friend.

I slam to a stop and jump out of the truck. The stables are coming to life around me with the sounds of morning that I've come to recognize and love—the huff and puff of hungry horses and the whinny of impatient ones, the clang of playful ones banging their halters against their doors, all punctuated by the meow of barn cats. I've even learned to love the smell.

I run as fast as I can to the back stables. Ever stands in the open doorway, waving frantically at me. I reach her side, and she grabs my hand to pull me farther in. She presses her finger to her lips to tell me to be quiet. Her engagement finger glints as it catches the light from the single sconce on the wall.

I follow her silently, amazed as I am every day that she's mine and I'm hers and this is all real—this life we're building. She runs the stables, and I run the club, and at night we plan our wedding and our future. When I first spotted her more than three years ago, I thought she was searching for that better fish in the sea. I was wrong. I was searching, and I found her.

We stop in front of an open stall where a laboring mare lays on a floor of hay. Stables employees and our veterinarian hover nearby.

Ever rises on her tiptoes and brings her lips to my ear. "She's almost there."

I wrap my arms around her from behind and draw her to my chest, resting my chin on her head.

A moment passes, and then I hear her voice.

Soft and sweetly off-tune.

Singing of freedom and Bobby McGee.

Until our little filly is born.

ALSO BY LYSSA KAY ADAMS

THE PROSPECT

One more summer. That's all 21-year-old Bree McTavish has left until she'll finally have enough money to get out of her seaside hometown where the only thing more famous than the rolling sand dunes dotting the shoreline are the Silver Lake Sluggers. Every June, the nation's top college baseball players descend on her tiny Michigan town to chase their big-time dreams in front of fans and Major League scouts. And every August, they leave behind a trail of broken hearts and mysterious stains in the bedrooms of the boarding house where Bree works as a cook to hone her skills for culinary school.

Bree hates summer. Hates baseball. Hates this tiny town.

If only she could hate *him*.

One more chance. Jax Tanner knows this is it—one last season of summer ball before his dreams of being a Major League draft pick dry up and scatter in the wind like the dunes of Silver Lake. Once a Top 20 prospect, he's now a wait-and-see thanks to a shoulder injury. If he doesn't literally hit a homerun this time—lots of them—the only baseball in his future might be the community rec team sponsored by his family's hardware chain. But baseball isn't Jax's only unfinished business in Silver Lake. There's also *her*. Bree McTavish. The sexy-as-hell girl who cooks for the team has bunted his every attempt at finding her sweet spot again after one hot night on the beach two years ago. He has no idea why she hates him so much, but he's not leaving until he finds out.

It's time for a new game plan.

One hot prospect. When a grand-slam of a secret is revealed, Bree realizes the only person she can fully trust is Jax. But when new opportunities arise, old fears intrude again. Can she learn to love the game, or will she lose her one hot prospect for true love when the Long Ball Boys pack up and leave with summer's end?

SEVENTH INNING HEAT

His career is on the line.

After a lackluster season and a disastrous performance that cost his team the World Series, Vegas Aces Pitcher Eric Weaver now faces an ultimatum from team management: Fix what's wrong with his game by the end of spring training, or else. When they tell him they're bringing in a new pitching coach to tweak his technique, he grits his teeth and agrees to be coached like a Little Leaguer again. He has sacrificed everything for his career and will do whatever it takes to save it. Until they tell him who the new coach is.

Her career is finally taking off.

Nicki Bates has worked her entire life to achieve one goal—to land a top coaching job in the Majors. But when she finally gets the call she's been waiting for, she realizes Fate has a sick sense of humor. The only team willing to take a chance on her is Eric Weaver's? Seven years ago, he dumped her cold when the Aces called him up from the minor leagues, and she vowed then she would never let something like love distract her from her goals again.

But when secrets from the past are revealed, the lingering sparks between them reignite into a fiery passion neither can ignore.

Will the heat destroy everything they've worked for? Or will a second chance at love prove the greatest victory of all?

Enjoy an excerpt from The Prospect!

~

PROLOGUE

Two summers ago

JAX TANNER

She dances on the shore, a lone dark shape against the moon-lit lake, a silhouette hidden by the shifting swell of the sand.

From the top of the dunes, I see the massive bonfire rising from the beach a hundred yards away, illuminating the throbbing surge of drunken, dancing teenagers who graduated from the local high school earlier in the day, including her.

She's one of them but not. She stands apart. Alone.

I'm not supposed to be here. None of my teammates are. The rules are strict when you're a first-year player for the Silver Lake Sluggers—the elite summer baseball team for the nation's best college players like me. Curfew is at midnight and underage drinking is forbidden. You break the rules, and you're out. No questions asked.

It sucks to think about spending my summer like a monk, but it's such a fucking privilege to be invited to play for the Sluggers—or any team in the prestigious Mackinac League—that we put up with the restrictions. Just putting on a Sluggers uniform sends your stock soaring and tells the entire baseball world you're the real deal.

A Major League hopeful.

A *prospect.*

But here I am, on the verge of breaking the rules, cresting one of the famous Silver Lake sand dunes with midnight less than an hour away, because I heard *she* would be here. The girl who works in the kitchen at the team boarding house.

The one who has been shooting me shy smiles for two weeks while she refills the salad bowl or brushes past me in the dining room. The one whose golden-brown eyes shimmer with a sadness she can never fully conceal. The one whose hips now sway to her own hypnotic rhythm that sucks me in like a powerful rip-tide.

Her arms are aloft in a graceful arch over her head. Her long, dark hair blows in the breeze. A beer loosely dangles from her fingertips, forgotten, an after-thought. Like the entire beach party raging without her in the distance.

Sand fills my shoes as I descend the hill. My teammates leave me in search of their own diversions, but I head for her. Only her.

"Bree," I say, testing her name like wistful oath on the breeze.

She turns, arms falling to her sides and her beer dropping to the wet ground at her feet. Her eyes widen and her lips part. I should probably say something, anything, but I can't.

"You're not supposed to be here," she blurts.

"I know," I laugh.

"You'll get trouble if they catch you."

"I know."

"Then why are you…"

Her question disappears on a gentle "oh" as I extend my hand. She stares at it with cautious longing—the same expression I catch on her face when she thinks I'm not paying attention. But I am. I always am.

Bree slowly reaches out. I fold her fingers in mine and tug her closer.

I might be a fool for being here.

For breaking the rules.

For risking everything.

But when she locks her eyes with mine and gives me that shy smile, I know it's going to be worth it.

The right girl always is.

CHAPTER ONE
Two summers later

BREE MCTAVISH

"Give me that bra, or I swear to God, I'll cook you."

This is how it's going to end for me.

In a face-off with a ten-pound ball of white fluff and sass. Everything I've worked for, every hour spent learning the ropes in a hot kitchen, every moment spent sweating the small stuff in my bank account until it's just big enough to get out of this town. *Poof.* It's all going to disappear because of this hoarding, mocking thief who's smirking at me because knows she can get away with it. She's the pampered, pink-bow-wearing princess of the boarding house owner whose goodwill can change in the blink of an eye, and I'm nothing but a cook who can be sent me packing just as fast.

I swear she plans these things, this dog. It's like she lays in wait for me to turn my back so she can dart underfoot at just the wrong moment to force me to spill a bowl of carefully washed cherries or knock over a tray of fresh muffins.

Or, in this case, so she can dart into the butler's pantry and emerge with evidence of my secret behind the shelves of canned tomatoes, pancake mixes, and apocalypse-sized jars of Crisco.

I love dogs. I do. If I didn't have my heart set on a career as a professional chef, I'd do something with animals. Because I love them.

Just not this one.

And definitely not today. Because today is *the* day. The day the

Sluggers move back into Edsel House for another summer of stealing bases and hearts. The day my hometown loses its damn mind over the aptly nicknamed Long Ball Boys.

The day *he* returns for his last summer here.

I should be rushing through my prep work for tomorrow's team breakfast so I can escape to a safe hiding space and start the humiliating process of avoiding Jax Tanner for another three long months.

But what am I doing instead? I'm chasing Matilda—and yeah, that's her real name—around the stainless-steel counters and appliances of the massive, professional-grade kitchen to retrieve the embarrassingly small scrap of faded pink lace now caught in her teeth.

Matilda skids to her right, and I try to grab her, but I realize too late it was a fake. The damn dog wants to pickle. She veers left around the prep counter and toward the door.

It suddenly swings open from the other side. I see my non-existent career flash before my eyes as I imagine Mrs. Armitage, owner of the house, or Mrs. C—the head chef—walking in.

Instead, I let out a relieved breath as my best friend, Lexi Acevedo, strolls in. "Shut the door!" I squawk.

Lexi nearly drops the paper bag in her arms, whips around and grabs the handle to stop the door from swinging. Matilda growls, races between her legs, and picks up the chase again.

"What the hell is going on?" Lexi laughs, setting the bag on the prep island in the center of the kitchen. The bag tips, and a bundle of fresh asparagus tumbles out with a clump of dirt, fresh from her mom's garden.

I run to the door and stand in the jamb, arms and legs splayed to block anyone else form coming in. "She stole my bra!"

Lexi looks under the counter and bursts out laughing. "How did she get your bra?"

"I did a load of laundry here," I lie, instantly feeling guilty for the deception.

"At least she didn't grab your underwear."

"Get one of her treats and see if she'll come to you."

"Right," she snorts. "That dog hates me as much as she hates you."

True. Lexi and I have both been working at Edsel House since the summer before our senior year in high school, and Matilda has treated us the entire time like a couple of hussies after her boyfriend. She's a bona fide mean girl. If she could shove us in front of a bus, she would.

But the men? Oh, she's a little doggie whore around them. The instant a Slugger comes within twenty feet of her, she's on her back, showing her belly, begging for love. And they fall for it every time. Every muscled alpha male on the team turns into a slobbering ball of mush over that damn dog.

Who has now inched out from under the counter to taunt me.

The little brat planned this just for today. I know it.

Lexi rises and shoots me a look over her shoulder. "Just stop chasing her. She'll let go of it the minute it stops being a game."

"It's not a game to her. She wants to ruin me."

Lexi makes a cuckoo noise and starts unpacking her bag. "My mom wants to know if you need any more morels. She's taking another tour out tomorrow morning."

I abandon my blockade of the door with a strong glare at Matilda. "If she can find them this late in the season, I'll cook them."

Lexi's mom owns a local hair salon but moonlights as a morel mushroom hunter, which sounds whacko to most people but not when you're from around here. This part of Michigan is a tourist destination for foodies who savor the nutty-flavored fungus that grows in the soggy forest floors just after the spring thaw.

"So..." Lexi says too casually, running asparagus under the water in the sink.

"Don't say it," I grumble.

"I saw him when I was walking in." "I told you not to say it."

"He looks good."

Of course, he does. He couldn't *not* look good. He's the *satisfaction guaranteed* of hotness, and ever since the night of my graduation, I've had to suffer his sexiness every summer as punishment for my own stupidity and reckless dreaming.

I was kind of hoping he wouldn't come this year.

Yet I'm shamefully giddy that he did.

Because I'm fifty shades of fucked up over Jax Tanner.

Just one more reason I can't wait to get out of Silver Lake, my tiny hometown where the only thing more famous than the blowing sand of the dunes is the annual antics of the Sluggers. They didn't get the nickname "The Long Ball Boys" for nothing.

Girls who grow up here learn two unbreakable lessons: how to properly cook morels and how not to drop your panties to a Long Baller.

I mastered the first one at an early age.

Too bad I had to learn the second one the hard way.

But I only have three more months of this, and then I'll have enough money to get out. Lansing—Michigan's capital city— awaits with its renowned community college culinary program. It's not exactly *Le Cordon Bleu*, but when you're a girl with no connections and zero money to her name, you have to start somewhere.

And I've been working my ass off for a long, long time to start there.

"He's, like, different or something," Lexi continues, gently shaking the asparagus of excess water and me of my wandering thoughts.

"Different how?"

She shrugs. "Bigger. Or maybe taller. I don't know. It's just *something*. It's like he went from hot college boy to *holy shit, he's a man* in a single year. You'll have to see for yourself."

"I'm going to try not to."

Lexi gives me a knowing smile and adopts a sing-song voice. "He has a beard."

My lady parts clench. A beard on Jax Tanner? Fate really does hate me.

"Not, like, one of those gross long ones," Lexi says, and we both shudder, because while the rest of the world may have fallen in love with that whole lumbersexual thing, we've grown up around national forest rangers who need to keep their faces warm in the winter, and we know for a fact how unsanitary that shit is.

"It's one of those sexy short ones that you can't tell if he grew on purpose or just got too lazy to shave for a while," Lexi continues. "Like the kind you want to just scratch with your fingernails."

I know the kind she's talking about, and picturing it on Jax's cut-from-glass jawline has me fanning myself.

Lexi snorts. "Exactly."

Matilda races toward me again, trying to get back in the game. I take Lexi's advice and ignore her. Matilda starts shaking my bra like she's trying to kill it, and she'll probably succeed. It's a Meijer Super Store clearance special that only has a few more washes in it before total disintegration.

Which feels like a sad a metaphor for my life.

On that happy thought, I bundle the freshly cleaned asparagus with some loose kitchen twine and prop it in a shallow dish of water. Best way to keep it fresh for tomorrow night's dinner.

Lexi returns to the prep counter to clean up the dirt. "Oh," she says, stopping to dig into her pocket. She pulls out a folded yellow paper. "Mom also wanted me to tell you that you're entering this year, no matter what, and if you say no, she's never going to give you another mushroom again."

I take the paper and shove it into my own pocket without looking at it. I know what it is. It's the entry form for the annual recipe contest at the upcoming International Asparagus Festival, which is actually a thing because *Michigan.*

Lexi side-eyes me on the way back to the sink. "The judges are big-time this year. You could get noticed by someone important!"

"I'll think about it."

"But the deadline is in two days!"

"So, I'll think about it until then."

Lexi plants her hands on her hips and gives me the look—the one she's been giving me since middle school when she knows I'm holding something back. That look has gotten me to confess way too much over the years, which is why I'm looking everywhere but at her right now. The secret I'm hiding today is as humiliating as the one she got out of me our junior year in high school. I can't risk it. She'll tell her mom again, and her mom will want to help. Again. I already owe them both too much.

"You know you're good enough to win, Bree," Lexi says.

"I know." I'm not being conceited. I'm talented in the kitchen, especially for someone with no formal training. Desperation is an efficient tutor. I've even started picking up gigs as a local wedding caterer on top of my work at the Edsel House. The extra money is the only reason I'm going to be able to get out of this town at the end of the summer instead of working another two years here.

But just barely, which is why the contest is once again not going to happen. I don't have an extra two hundred and fifty dollars lying around to cover the entry fee.

Lexi lets out a drawn-out sigh like she's about to lecture me, but she cuts it off when we hear the voice.

His voice.

In the dining room and coming closer.

I can't make out the words, but it sounds like he's on the phone with someone. I hear the deep timbre of his low laugh, and a cold shiver races up my spine as I imagine a hot blonde on the other side of the call. Or a hot brunette. Or just any other girl, because he could totally have a girlfriend and probably does by now. And I hate myself for caring.

I close my eyes and swallow as an entire jungle of butterflies takes flight in my stomach.

Lexi slugs me on the arm. "Go out there and say hi," she hisses.

I slug back. "Shut up!"

"If you won't, I will."

She starts for the door. I grab her arm to hold her back, but she sticks her tongue out at me and pulls away.

I see disaster unfolding in slow motion, like one of those dreams where you need to run by can't get your feet to move.

Lexi plants her hand in the center of the swinging door.

"Lexi, wait!"

But it's too late. Matilda has spotted her escape. She races out from under the counter. The door starts to swing shut again, but Matilda manages to slip through the tiny sliver of opening and out of sight, straight into the dining room, my bra dangling from her mouth like a dead animal.

The only thing more embarrassing than the sound of Jax Tanner's amused laughter as he greets the little bitch is the look on his face when he pushes the door open from the other side, my bra dangling from his fingers.

He holds it out and quirks an eyebrow over sexy, hooded eyes. "What exactly do you do in this kitchen, Bree?"

CHAPTER TWO

BREE

Lexi was right. He's different.

My brain tries to catalogue all the changes during the split-second suspension of time between my irrational dizziness at seeing him and my total humiliation at the circumstances.

He's bigger. Broader. He fills up the space in the doorway like a ... Well, like a full-grown *man*. Lexi was definitely right about that part. But it's not just his sheer size that has changed.

He swings the bra and cocks an eyebrow over mocking eyes.

Maybe that's what's different. He seems to be making fun of me. Though I have no reason to expect anything else from him—after all, I'm the one who ran away from him—it stings. We've been a lot of things to each other, but unkind has never been one of them.

I recover from my stupor long enough to stomp two steps closer and grab my bra. Matilda, who has settled between his feet like a she's guarding her prize, growls and bares her teeth.

Don't worry, dog. He's all yours.

Lexi clears her throat in a totally non-subtle way. "Hey, Jax," she chirps. "How was school this year?"

He glances her way with a blinding, flirty smile. "Good. You?"

"Great. It was, um, great." Lexi bites her lip and then swivels on her feet to stare at me. She bugs out her eyes at me as if to say, *Say something.*

"Did-did you need something?" I stammer.

He pats his rock hard abs. "Yeah, I'm starving. I missed dinner.

I was going to grab an apple or something, but then Matilda tried to give me a present." He stops and winks. *Winks*. Not in a meaningful way, either but a flirty way. I hate it. "Anyway, I figured it had to be yours. Don't suppose you have anything left over from dinner?"

"A little." *Figured it had to be yours.* It's only the bra I was wearing that night, but I don't suppose I can expect him to remember that. I don't *want* him to remember that. Ugh. I hate myself so much.

"Awesome. Mind if I fix a plate?"

I blink, stomach clenching. "I-I can do it."

"Really? Thanks."

He winks again, and the meaningless gesture makes heat rise on my skin. I walk toward the line of commercial, Sub-Zero refrigerators that take up nearly an entire wall of the kitchen. I avoid Lexi's gaze, because everything about this is humiliating. The way he's treating me. My bra. Everything.

I open the first fridge and pull out a stack of three dishes where I'd packed away the left-over chicken, mashed potatoes, and gravy. I set them on the prep counter and then retrieve a warm plate from the door-type dishwasher on the other side of the refrigerators.

"Looks awesome," he says, coming up next to me as I return to the prep counter. He peers over my shoulder. "I swear, you need to write a cookbook or something. You know that chicken dish you started making last year? The one with the cherries on top? I tried to make that for my girlfriend, but I didn't even come close."

Girlfriend. Oh. God. My hand shakes, and I dribble gravy on the counter as I transfer it from bowl to plate. Lexi is suddenly super busy doing absolutely nothing.

"Braised chicken thighs with cherry compote," I say.

"Yeah, that's the one."

I slide the plate in his direction without turning around. "You know where the forks are, right?" I say fighting to keep my voice steady. "You can use the microwave in the dining room."

He grabs the plate. "Thanks, Bree. You're the best."

And then he turns and walks back through the door.

My hands rest palms-down on the cold counter. I'm stunned into mute inertia.

Thanks, Bree. You're the best. Did he really just say that? After dropping the girlfriend bomb in my lap? The heat on my cheeks explodes from the mild burn of embarrassment to a raging inferno of mortification. In all my years working here, I've never felt more like the hired help than I do right now.

"Bree," Lexi sighs, waving a hand in front of my face from the other side of the counter.

I shake my head. "Don't."

"I'm sure it's not a serious girlfriend."

"He tried to make her a recipe." *My recipe.* "That's a serious girlfriend."

Lexi suddenly snaps. "Well, what the hell did you expect? You've been blowing him off for two years! Anyone would give up after that."

"I had sex with him," I blurt.

Lexi blinks so hard and fast that she looks like one of those annoying talking bird dolls we were so obsessed with as kids. The ones you had to tiptoe around when you got up in the middle of the night to pee because the slightest vibration would send it squawking awake for an hour.

"I'm sorry, I think I just hallucinated. Did you say you had sex with him? With Jax Tanner?!"

The last part came out a high-pitched squeak. I hiss at her. "Keep your voice down!"

Lexi rounds the counter and grabs my arm to shake me. "When the hell did this happen?" She doesn't wait for me to answer. I see the conclusion arrive in her eyes as she steps back. "Holy shit. The night on the beach. After graduation."

I nod, avoiding her eyes by repacking the left-overs.

"How could you not tell me?"

I stack the dishes. "I didn't want you to know."

"*Why?* You're my best friend! That's the whole point of having a best friend, so you have someone to tell when you lose your virginity to a hot guy on a beach!"

"I know, but—"

"I told you when I lost my virginity last summer! How could you not at least *mention* it?"

"Because I didn't want you to know what an idiot I am!"

Lexi sighs again and leans against the counter. She doesn't need me to clarify what I mean, because she knows. Lexi is walking, breathing proof of what happens when a local girl violates Rule #2. The town's favorite game next to baseball itself is guessing which Major League ball player is Lexi's father. Everyone knows she's the product of a summer fling between a local girl with stars in her eyes and a Long Baller with lust in his who took off at summer's end and never looked back.

That's probably why we became friends. We both walk around this town with giant gossip bulls-eyes on our backs. The only thing they love to talk about as much as the identity of Lexi's father is the shocking truth about mine. Which I seemed to be the only person in town who didn't know until the day we graduated.

"I've done what your mother asked. But you're done with school now, and you're no longer my responsibility."

I stared at the suitcase he dropped at my feet. The graduation cap slides off my head. "You're my father!"

"No, I'm not."

I shake off the memory. It doesn't matter. I'm over it. He was a shitty excuse even for a fake father, anyway.

"Bree, I wouldn't have judged you. Is that what you think?" Lexi asks.

I shrug and return the dishes to the fridge.

"I would never judge you! And anyway, he's not like the others. He's not like my sperm donor." That's what Lexi calls the man who fathered her. "Jax is a good guy. And he was so into you! Everyone could see it!"

I shove the dishes back in the fridge and turn around, arms crossed. "It doesn't matter now."

She leans against the counter and matches my pose. "So, what happened?"

"I basically threw myself at him."

Lexi covers her mouth with her hand, but not before I see her smile.

"Laugh, if you want, but it's true. It was all me. He invited me to go for a walk, we stopped to sit and talk in that little patch of birch trees by the house, and the next thing I know, we're going at it like monkeys."

Lexi laughs but stops herself. "I'm sorry. It's just so not you. Were you drunk?"

"No. Just—" I shrug and give her a pointed look. "You know."

"Upset," she says quietly. She was the one who picked me up after Brett—I refuse to think of him as dad or step-dad—threw me out with my meager belongings stuffed into that suitcase, the sting of his confession like a fresh, raw wound.

"So, was it, like, bad or something?"

It's my turn to laugh. "Uh, no. It was amazing." Perfect. Passionate. Romantic. What every girl dreams her first time will be like—a fairy tale under a full moon. But like any good fairy tale, the clock struck midnight.

"Then I don't understand why—"

"Because I used him," I say, cutting her off. "I wanted to feel something good. I wanted to feel *wanted*. But when it was over, I felt so … "

My voice trails off as I look down. I'm still too embarrassed to articulate it.

"Guilty?" she supplies.

I nod head and look up. "But also naïve. I knew better, you know? How many times did your mom warn us not to trust a Long Baller? I thought I was just using him for sex, but when it was over, I knew it wasn't going to be enough for me. I wanted more." I shrug. "So, I ran."

"Before he could run away from you."

I nod. "Yeah."

"He doesn't seem to be running, though. He's back for a third summer, Bree."

"With a *girlfriend*. He's not back for me." And even if he were, I'm smarter than that. Fairy tales aren't real.

Lexi closes the small distance between us and pulls me in for a tight hug. "I still can't believe you didn't tell me. I'm trying really hard to not hate you for that."

"I'm sorry." I squeeze my arms around her, guilt rising again because I'm hiding something else from her at the moment. "I just, you know…"

Lexi pulls away. "Yeah, I know, because I know *you*. And you'd think I was used to your secrets by now, but … " She shakes her head and sucks in a deep breath. She lets it out and heads for the door. "I gotta run. See you tomorrow night?"

Right. The annual pre-season team dinner. Lexi always helps

out as a cook and server. I nod and wave as she leaves. As soon as she's gone, I drop my face into my hands.

Three more months. That's all I have left until I can start over in a place where I don't need to hide behind secrets. Where I don't see the look of pity on every face I meet. Where I no longer dream of a Prince Charming and his fairy tale smile on a moonlit beach.

Three months.

And then I can finally start writing my own damn happy ending.

Want to read more? The Prospect is available until September 2017 in THE HOT ZONE box set and in print beginning Fall 2017.

∼

CHAPTER ONE

Eric Weaver rarely missed a pitch, but this was one curve ball he didn't see coming. And just like a line drive to the balls, it left him with a burning need to bend over and heave.

"You can't be serious."

His eyes darted back and forth between the two men before him. Las Vegas Aces owner Devin Dane sat behind his desk, feet up and arms crossed over his pansy-assed tie as if he hadn't just dropped a potentially career-ending bomb in Eric's lap. Team manager Hunter Kinsley stood on his right flank, looking like a slightly remorseful lieutenant who tried to talk his superiors out of shock-and-awe but followed orders anyway. Behind them both, the sinking St. Augustine sun streamed through the window and illuminated the Aces' spring training field in the distance.

This had to be a joke. Some kind of twisted, preseason prank, right? Eric waited for a signal, a flicker of a smart-assed grin or something that would indicate Hunter and Devin were just dicking him around.

Instead, they met his gaze head-on.

"Sonuvabitch." Disbelief sent the air from his lungs and the strength from his spine. He sank against the leather cushion of his chair.

They were talking about moving him to the bullpen. The

bullpen. After seven years as a starting pitcher, being busted down to the ranks of reliever would not only be a major demotion but also one cocksucker of a humiliation. He could see the blog posts already. *Eric Weaver, son of retired Texas Rangers pitcher Chet Weaver, could never live up to the legacy of his storied father.*

He shot to his feet. "You can't do this to me."

Devin tented his fingers beneath his chin. "It's not about you. It's about what's best for the team."

"Keeping me on the mound is what's best for this team." Even as Eric said it, though, self-doubt churned in his gut. For two years, he had felt the magic slipping away. It didn't matter how hard he worked, how much he trained and drilled. His curves fell flat. His fastballs lost their heat. And when it had mattered most, he failed in brutally spectacular fashion. Four months ago in the last game of the World Series, he gave up five home runs. His teammates would have championship rings if not for him.

But dammit, Devin and Hunter couldn't do this.

"Who—" Eric had to stop and clear his throat. "Who would take my place?"

"We're looking at Zach Nelson," Hunter said.

For fuck's sake. Talk about rubbing salt to a wound. Zach Nelson was an untested rookie known more for his lumberjack beard and his surfer-boy lifestyle than his prowess on the mound.

Eric couldn't let it happen. He wouldn't. "What do I have to do?"

"You need to work your ass off these next six weeks and do everything your coaches tell you." He tossed a plain manila folder onto the desk. "Especially that one."

"Who is that?"

Hunter straightened and crossed his arms across his chest.

"We're bringing on a new pitching coach, Eric. One with a reputation for kicking asses and whipping people back into shape. We think she'll be good for you."

Eric blinked as one key word sank in. "S*he*?"

CHAPTER TWO

There was only one *she* anywhere in the United States Eric could think of who met Hunter's description and was even remotely qualified to be a pitching coach for a Major League Baseball team.

There was no way his luck was that bad.

Eric stared at the folder a moment before swiping it off the desk. He opened it and felt the world tilt beneath his feet.

Correction: His luck was that bad.

He actually felt dizzy as he met Devin's gaze. "You have to be kidding me."

"It's just a new coach," Devin said, smirking. "What's the big deal?"

A new coach he could handle. Hell, he'd sign himself up for Little League again if it meant ending the two-year shit spiral that had stolen the velocity from his fastball and turned his curve into a flat-line meatball.

But Devin and Hunter weren't bringing on just any coach.

They were bringing on *Nicki Bates*.

Sweet jeezus.

Devin dropped his feet to the floor. "You seem bothered by this. I'm surprised. Didn't you and her brother play together at Vanderbilt? I thought you were friends."

Eric snorted. *Friends.* He dropped the folder back on the desk. "This is a disaster waiting to happen."

"Because she's a woman?" Hunter said. "She's more qualified than ninety percent of the coaches in the bigs right now."

"It's not because she's a woman!"

Devin raised his eyebrows. "Then what's the problem?"

Eric jerked his fingers through his hair and swallowed

against a cocktail of surging anger and simmering lust. The first one was a feeling he was well acquainted with these days. But the second was an emotion he thought he'd doused long ago. His mind called up the image of her. Long limbs. Seductive eyes. Lips that could make a man's imagination head straight for the foul line.

That was the problem. He couldn't be within fifty feet of her without wanting to *conference on the mound*. It was a distraction he couldn't afford, not if he wanted to save his spot in the rotation.

He couldn't explain any of that to Devin or Hunter, though. The one and only promise he'd ever managed to keep to her was never to tell a soul about them, and he wasn't about to break it now. He was already having a hard time looking at himself in the mirror these days.

Devin and Hunter stared at him with matching smirks, waiting for his response.

He searched for something that sounded at least plausible. "We can't take this kind of attention right now, Devin. The guys were barely talking to each other at the end of last season, and this is going to only make things worse."

"I realize the media coverage will be intense. The first woman ever to coach for a Major League ball club is going to bring a lot of scrutiny."

"It'll be a fucking circus."

"That's where you come in. The players respect you and will follow your lead. You're still the team captain."

For now. The unspoken threat hung in the air. No relief pitcher would ever be chosen by his peers as team captain.

Devin suddenly stood. "The deal is done, Eric. We're announcing her tomorrow morning. She's already here."

Shit. He'd spent the better part of seven years doing everything in his power to stay as far away as possible from her. And now here she was.

Same state.

Same city.

Same fucking team.

"Where is she staying?" He barely got the words out.

Hunter cocked an eyebrow. "Going to welcome her to the team?"

"Something like that."

Devin rounded his desk. "We put her up in the four-thirty-two house."

Eric stalked across the office and threw open the door. It crashed against the opposite wall as he stormed into the hallway. Nicki's talent was unmistakable, but her presence on the team would only bring trouble. If he was going to save his career, he needed absolute focus on one thing and one thing only: the game.

That would be impossible with Nicki anywhere near him.

Which left him with only one certainty.

Nicki Bates had to go.

***

Eric whipped his Escalade into the only available spot on the street and groaned. Five other cars were parked in front of the house where Nicki was staying.

That could only mean one thing.

Her family was there.

But why wouldn't they be there? This was the culmination of her life's work, the realization of a dream she'd had since she'd first put on a ball glove as a kid. Eric should have expected them to be there to celebrate with her. But their presence wasn't going to make this any easier. Eric couldn't wait, though. Not if Devin was determined to announce her to the world in the morning. He had to make her see reason before then.

He crossed the street and walked up the brick pathway toward the door. The house was a smallish ranch with palm trees out front and a lawn full of that spiky green shit that passed for grass in Florida. In Eric's seven years with the Aces, the house had been home to everyone from marketing temps to college prospects. And now Nicki.

Sweet jeezus.

The closer he got, the louder the noise grew. The Bates family had no concept of inside voice. They yelled. They fought. They ran with scissors. Nicki was the youngest of four and the only girl. As an only child, Eric had always felt like he'd walked into a sitcom whenever Robby invited him home from school.

It felt more like walking into The Godfather this time.

Seven years had passed since he'd been welcomed into the family. Though Robby played for the Red Sox and they saw each other on the field several times a year, they barely spoke. Some betrayals couldn't be overcome.

Eric rang the doorbell and waited, hands in the pockets of his jeans.

A few seconds passed before the door swung open.

Ah, shit. "Robby-"

Nicki's brother let out a growl and threw a punch. It connected with Eric's mouth before he had time to duck. Eric stumbled back, his hand covering his now-throbbing jaw. He pulled his fingers away and swore at the blood. "What the hell, man?"

Robby stormed out the door. "I warned you."

"The fuck you did."

"I told you if you ever came near her again, I would beat your ass."

Eric dabbed at the blood again. "Well, in case you haven't heard, she's apparently now my coach. It's going to be a little difficult to stay away from her."

He should've known Robby would be there. The first few days of spring training were only for pitchers and catchers. As a first baseman, Robby wouldn't have to head to the Red Sox training facility in Fort Myers for at least a week. Just fucking great.

"Robby? What is all the commotion?"

Nicki's mom appeared in the doorway. "Oh my goodness. Eric, dear." Her Italian accent was as strong as ever. "Robby, why didn't you tell us he was here? Eric, dear, come inside. Are you staying for dinner? Are you bleeding? What happened?"

Robby glared one more time before moving aside to let his mother grab Eric's hand and pull him in. "Oh, Eric, I'm so glad you are here. Isn't this wonderful? You and Nicki on the same team."

Yeah. Wonderful.

She pulled him into a living room with furniture that had seen its fair share of shenanigans. There was a rumor that a college prospect had even lost his virginity on the couch. *Note to self: Don't sit down.*

Sliding glass doors on the far end of the room opened onto a patio and a fenced-off pool. Through the glass, Eric spotted Nicki's two other brothers, two women he didn't recognize, and some children that hadn't existed the last time he'd been around. Her father stood over a flaming grill poking meat with a giant fork.

"How many steaks do you want, dear?"

Eric found his voice. "Thank you, Mrs. Bates, but—"

"Isabella. How many times do you I have to tell you to call me Isabella?" She pinched his cheek. The throbbing one. "All these years, and you're still so polite."

"*Isabella*. Thank you. But I just came by to talk to Nicki. I can't stay for dinner."

"No. You will eat."

Robby grunted. Or growled. It was hard to tell the difference.

Eric ignored him. "Is Nicki here?"

"Of course, dear. She'll be out in a minute. She's in the shower."

Great. Just the image he needed—Nicki, wet and soapy.

The sliding glass doors suddenly opened and her father walked in. He stopped short, and Eric waited for another blow to the face. Instead, Andrew Bates smiled and held out his arms.

"Eric. It's good to see you, boy."

Eric let the man pull him in for hearty back-pounding hug. Robby let out another indecipherable noise.

Isabella smacked his arm. "What is wrong with you, Robby? Is that any way to treat an old friend?"

That answered one question he'd always had. Did her parents ever know about them? No, apparently.

Isabella brushed past him toward a hallway that led to the bedrooms. "I will go see what's taking our Nicki so long."

Just when she disappeared around the corner, the sliding glass doors opened again. Andrew walked back out to the grill as Nicki's other brothers—Vincent and Anthony—walked in. They joined Robby in an offensive line of crossed arms and glowering stares that would've made any NFL team proud.

That answered the other question. Her other brothers *did* know. Great.

They glared for a long moment while Eric glanced around the

room. This was ridiculous. They were all adults here. Couldn't they behave like it?

He looked at Robby. "When you going to Fort Myers?"

"Don't talk to me."

"Gotcha."

Eric shoved his hands back in his pockets and looked at his feet. Somewhere down the hallway, a door opened and closed. Isabella appeared and smiled. "She's almost ready."

A minute later, Nicki walked out.

And Eric went dumb.

She was even more gorgeous now than she had been at twenty-two. Her skin glowed like a damn skin care commercial, and her long, dark hair hung wet across her shoulders. She wore a white Aces t-shirt that left little to the imagination about the curves and well-honed muscles underneath. Her long legs were encased in beat-up jeans that hugged her in all the right places and made him want to drop to his knees and thank God for creating the thing called woman. *This* woman, in particular.

His tongue was thick in his mouth. "Hey."

She tossed him a smile, but it was meaningless—the kind reserved for players you only saw a couple times every season.

"Eric, hey. I'm glad you're here. I was going to call you tonight to go over a few things before tomorrow, because we really need to get started as soon as possible. What the hell happened to your face?"

Eric blinked. She was staring at him like he was supposed say something. "What?"

"Your face—" She groaned and glared at her brothers over his shoulder. "What did you do?"

"I warned him," Robby said.

She shook her head and refocused on Eric. "Do you want some ice?"

"Do I need ice?"

"You're starting to swell."

He touched his jaw and winced. "Can we talk in private, please?"

"No." That was from Anthony, who had moved to stand next to Nicki as if she needed protection.

The door to the back yard slid open again, and her father leaned his head in. "Eric, medium for your steaks? Or you like 'em a little more done?"

Nicki pulled a phone from her pocket and swiped the screen a couple of times. "Give me your email address. I need to send you a schedule of the new workouts."

He blinked again. "New workouts?"

"Eric, medium or well-done?"

Nicki looked at her dad. "He likes them pink in the middle."

"I'm not staying for dinner."

Nicki returned her attention to Eric. "Your email address?"

Isabella yelled from the kitchen. "Eric, what kind of dressing do you like on your salad, dear?"

"Um—"

"Just oil and vinegar for him, Mom. He needs to take some weight off."

What?!

"Butter and sour cream on your potato, dear?"

"Mom, I'm putting him on a diet. No sour cream."

Eric looked down at his stomach. He didn't need to lose weight. Sure, he'd been eating like shit lately and maybe he had gotten a little softer than his usual playing shape, but.... dammit. "Nicki, I need to talk to you. *Now.*"

"Great." She turned the phone so he could see the screen. "This is a schedule of—"

"You have to quit."

The words were out of his mouth before he could even think about pulling them back in.

Another fist met his face.

There were some gasps, a few yells, and one loud curse—which probably came from him—as he toppled and landed with a thud on his back.

Anthony leaned over him with a steely glare, his fist ready for another throw. He'd played football at Ohio State and majored in meathead. He was now apparently making a career out of it.

Nicki pushed him away. "Oh my God. Will you guys please stop trying to break the merchandise?"

"Did you just call me *merchandise*?"

Nicki crouched next to him on the floor. "You arm is worth eighty million dollars. You're merchandise."

He grabbed her hand. "Nicki, I really, really, really need to talk to you alone."

Nicki swallowed and sighed. "Fine."

She stood, offered her hand, and helped him to his feet. Just holding her fingers in his was like a hundred Red Bulls to his system. If she felt the same jolt, she hid it well.

She headed back down the hallway, holding up a hand to stop her brothers from following. "Give us a few minutes, guys."

They grunted in unison.

He followed Nicki into a room at the end of the hallway that looked like some kind of home office. She swung the door shut behind him and then crossed her arms. "Well?"

Seven years. That's how long it had been since he'd been alone in a room with her. The realization brought his brain to a halt.

She cocked her head and raised her eyebrows. The move brought his attention to a small scar above her left eye that hadn't been there the last time he saw her.

"I believe you were saying something about me quitting," she deadpanned.

Right. That. "We both know this is a bad idea, Nicki."

"I think it's a great idea, actually. I'm living the dream."

"I'm talking about us!"

"There is no us."

"Nicki—"

"But I'm glad you brought it up, because there is something I want to discuss with you." She uncrossed her arms and settled her hands on her hips. "Your promise still stands, I hope."

"Don't worry, sweetheart. Except for your brothers out there, I'm still your dirty little secret."

"Good. Because I'm sure you can see how uncomfortable it would make things for me if people knew about our little fling."

"*Little fling?*"

"Should I call it something else?"

"It was a helluva lot more than that, and you know it."

She snorted. "Which one of us are you trying to convince?"

"You of the selective memory."

"My memory is perfectly clear. I especially remember the part when you disappeared."

Bam! Nicki could throw a verbal fastball as powerful as the real thing, and this one hit its target. He had to fight the urge to rub his chest even as he admired her aim. She was the only woman he'd ever known who wasn't afraid to knock him off his pedestal. In a different situation, he might even enjoy the sparring. But there was too much at stake now, and Eric was an all-star competitor.

He closed the distance between them and lowered his voice. "I get it now. This is revenge. I dumped you, so now you're getting back at me."

To his surprise, Nicki tipped her head back and let out a booming laugh. "Yeah," she gasped in between guffaws. "I orchestrated this entire thing just to get back at you." She smirked. "I hate to burst your bubble, Eric, but it really wasn't that good."

Bam! Fastball number two. This one whipped past his bat and landed with a humiliating thud in the catcher's mitt. He shook it off and stepped back up to the plate. "You know what? You're a rotten liar. Because I seem to recall you calling my name over and over again."

"And I seem to recall faking it a lot."

Bam! Fastball number three. This one nailed him in the head. Which meant it was time to charge the mound. "I don't think so, darlin'."

He moved toward her. She backed up until she collided with the wall. He planted his hands on either side of her head.

His eyes dropped to her lips, and that was all it took. Blood rushed to his groin as memories came back in carnal clarity. Her body beneath his. Her eyes closed. Her voice calling his name.

Shit. Whatever he thought he was starting, it was something else now. Because when he tore his gaze from her mouth back to her eyes, he could barely remember what they'd been fighting about. He didn't know what the fuck came over him—the casual dismissal in her eyes, the smell of her skin, the memories suddenly slamming him from every direction.

She cocked an eyebrow. "What are you doing?"

"Jogging your memory."

Eric claimed her lips.

And felt an explosion of pain as her knee met his nuts.

He doubled over with an oomph just as her hands shoved at his shoulders and sent him reeling. He stumbled backwards and then fell to his knees. He couldn't breathe. Couldn't talk but for a single, guttural groan. His hands covered his junk and he fell forward. If he ever hoped to have children, he was pretty sure that dream had just died.

Her feet appeared in front of his face. "Don't ever do that again."

He tugged one hand free from under his body and managed a thumbs up.

"Are you all right?"

He mumbled into the carpet. "I think you broke it."

"Do you want some ice now?"

He thought about asking her to kiss it for him, but he liked his life, thank you very much.

"Look at me, Eric."

He moaned and rolled onto his back. She glared down at him. He immediately pictured her naked, and his dick twitched in response. Thank God it still worked.

"You think I don't know what you're doing?"

Shit. Was it that obvious?

"You think you can kiss me and touch me and I'll just come running after you?" She didn't give him time to respond. "You nearly derailed me from my dreams once. I won't let you do it again."

He pushed himself off the floor and stood, swallowing away a wave of nausea as his balls dropped from his throat. "What are you talking about? I always supported you."

"I almost gave it all up for you. Remember that?" Her voice took on a mocking tone. "*I don't know if I can do this without you, Nicki. I almost left school for you!* And then you dumped me, thank God."

She jabbed him in the chest. "I'm not the stupid girl I used to be, Eric. You might have hurt me back then, but you leaving me was the best thing that ever happened to me. And do you know why? Because you taught me a lesson I've never forgotten, a lesson that has gotten me here."

"What lesson is that?"

"The game is all that matters."

She wasn't even bothering with fastballs anymore. She was full-on cheating. Throwing in the dirt. Wiping pine tar on the ball.

And it worked. He was out. For now. "Are we done here, *coach*?"

"We're done."

She stepped around him and jerked open the door. He wanted to stomp behind her, but he had to settle for limping to the living room. Isabella, oblivious to the tension radiating between them, passed him a plate covered with tin foil.

"Robby told me you're not staying, so I put your food here. You can take it with you."

"Thank you, but I—"

She shoved it at him. "You eat."

Nicki smirked as he accepted the plate. He tried to smile at Isabella, but that only further cracked open the corner of his mouth. He winced and dabbed at the bleeding with his tongue. How the hell was he going to explain his face to the guys on the team?

Nicki marched to the front door and swung it open wide.

He walked outside and turned around. "Nicki—"

"Batter up, babe."

She slammed the door in his face.

CHAPTER THREE

Sometimes Fate was hell bent on kicking a man when he was down. Eric felt the blow of Her steel-toed snake skins as soon as he pulled into his driveway and saw the Ford truck with Texas plates blocking his garage. He had just enough fight left in him to consider ramming it with his Escalade, but he also had just enough throb left in his groin to subdue the urge.

Eric found him in the kitchen, stirring something on the stove. In the two years since they'd last spoken, his hair had faded into the color of a stormy sky and the small paunch he'd developed early in retirement was once again flat with athletic tautness.

Eric glanced around the room. The tower of pizza boxes was gone. The sink was empty of the dirty dishes that had been piling up for a week. The stench of laziness had been replaced by a lemony clean aroma. The place was goddamned spotless.

Eric dropped the plate from Isabella on the counter. Chet Weaver turned around as if that were the first he'd noticed Eric's arrival.

"Hello, son."

"How'd you get in here?"

"You gave us a key."

"I gave *Mom* a key."

Chet nodded toward the pot. "I kept it warm for you."

Eric snorted. "You don't expect me to believe you cooked, do you?"

His father faked a chuckle. "I got pretty good at it when your mother was sick."

Eric clenched his jaw and stormed to the fridge. He threw open the door and stared inside, searching for a beer that wasn't there. It took him a second to realize that he was looking at fresh produce and full gallons of milk. Things that hadn't been there this morning.

Eric slammed the door and whipped around. "What is this? What are you doing here?"

"Your mother used to help you get ready for the season. I thought I would, too."

"Mom was invited. You're not."

"Just the same."

Chet was refusing to take the bait. His tone suggested a practiced patience, like an umpire standing stone-faced in front of an unhinged manager. It made Eric want to throw things. He didn't need this. Not now. Not today. Hell, not *ever*.

"I want you gone tomorrow."

"Fair enough. But why don't you at least sit down for a few minutes and tell me what happened to your face."

"I ran into some fists."

"Wanna talk about it?"

"With you? Fuck no."

Chet showed the first signs of life. He rolled his lips in and out as if he were literally biting his tongue.

Eric tried to summon some satisfaction but couldn't find it. He shook his head and headed toward the hallway on the other side of the kitchen. "I'm going to my room. Be gone in the morning."

"It's time to end this, Eric. It's been long enough."

"Maybe for you."

"Eric—"

His father's voice faded away as Eric rounded the corner and trudged upstairs. The world had a sick sense of humor. In the span of one hour, the two people he most needed to stay in his past had parked themselves front and center in his life.

Eric emptied his pockets onto his dresser, avoiding the mirror on the wall. If he looked up and studied his reflection, he would barely recognize the face staring back at him. He'd see his mother's green eyes, his father's square jaw, and a dark complexion that hinted at a Sioux ancestry. But they were all just pieces. Parts thrown together in a puzzle that used to fit, back when he still knew who he was and what he wanted. Back when the ball felt right in his hand and he could control his entire world from a mound of dirt.

Long enough? Not even close.

Not with Nicki.

Not with his father.

Not by a long shot.

***

Chet let out the breath he'd been holding as his one and only child walked away. Again.

He turned off the stove and reminded himself that he'd never believed this would be easy. He'd also known it was risky— surprising him like this—but desperate times called for desperate measures. What was it his counselor in rehab used to say? *It won't be easy, but it will be worth it.*

There was a special kind of torture in knowing your child was hurting. It was even worse knowing it was your fault.

But, hey, Chet had managed to wrangle one night out of it. Score one for Dad.

In the morning, he'd figure out how to convince Eric to let him stay the week. Then all of spring training. Then he'd find a way to let Eric know he'd rented an apartment in Vegas and had purchased season tickets.

Chet covered the pot and carried it to the fridge. Chicken noodle soup always tasted better the next day, anyway. He hoped it was still Eric's favorite. A good father would know for sure, but Chet had never been that.

He heard the sound of running water upstairs, as if Eric had turned on the shower. It was barely seven o'clock. Eric had made it clear he was going to stay in his room all night, which certainly wasn't the worst outcome Chet could have imagined. Eric could have tossed him out on his ass. He could have called the cops. Or he could have repeated the last words he'd spoken to Chet two years ago after the funeral.

"She was the only good part of this family, and now she's gone. And there is absolutely no point in you and I pretending to be anything other than strangers."

"I'm your father."

"Took you a little too long to figure that out."

Eric was right. It had taken Chet too long. Too many years wasted—figuratively and literally. Too many years when he thought the game was the most important thing in his life; that the people he loved most would simply be there when it was all gone. Too many years assuming they understood why he did the things he did; that the pressure of being Chet Weaver justified the women, the booze, the yelling. Too many years thinking the best way to show his love for his son was to push him hard to succeed.

He always believed he would have time later to make up for the shit storm he rained down on his wife and son.

He was wrong.

Chet let out a breath and wiped the counter one last time with a wet cloth, scrubbing away the miniscule remnants of the disturbing mess he'd found when he arrived. His son had never been a slob. Eric was meticulous, disciplined.

But crumb by crumb, stain by stain, Chet would scrub until the slate was clean.

Whatever Eric threw at him, he was ready to catch. He was prepared to go all nine innings and then some if necessary.

Because a man will do just about anything to get his son back.

Want to read more? Seventh Inning Heat is available on Amazon, Barnes and Noble, and iBooks!

ABOUT LYSSA

Lyssa Kay Adams is the pen name of an award-winning journalist who gave up the world of telling true stories to pen emotional romances. She's also a diehard Detroit Tigers fan who will occasionally cheer for the Red Sox because her husband is from Boston.

Lyssa lives in Michigan with her family and an anxiety-ridden Maltese who steals food and buries it around the house. Including in Lyssa's bed.

You can keep up with Lyssa at LyssaKayAdams.com or on Twitter at @LyssaKayAdams.

ACKNOWLEDGMENTS

A book is never the work of one person. An author relies on the help, guidance, and comforting shoulders of many people to bring a story to life.

Huge thanks to my family, first and foremost, for putting up with the insanity of living with a full-time author.

And a major shout-out to the writing friends who have helped me and inspired me along the way. To my original critique group – Mary, Jennifer, Dana, Michelle, and Paula. You will always be my "girls in the basement." Further thanks to my Romance Writers of America friends: Jennifer Lyon, Marianne Donley, Alyssa Alexander, and so many more that it would take an entire book to list them all. Special thanks to Christina Mitchell and Meika Usher for the writing binges, the wine, and the laughs. And to my "binders." Thank you. You keep me sane.

And finally, to Michelle Baty, designer rock star... I got you hooked on romance novels. Don't try to deny it.